Finnish Tango

Boško Velimirović

Original title: Finski tango

Translation from Serbian to English by Ana Popović

Edited by David Chudoba

CONTENTS

Introduction

Body and Smile

A small man, dressed in old-fashioned clothes came on board. He pulled his hat all the way down to his eyebrows to prevent it from flying off with the gusts of wind. He wondered if he would survive falling from the deck into the sea, as if he could feel that he would fall eventually. But his fall would happen during winter when there would be no chance of survival. The small man's name was Joni. Joni had small ambitions, both in friendship and love, but he had luck with one thing, at least for a short while – he stole the love of the protagonist of this story. This is why we are mentioning him now. Alone in the midst of a noisy crowd he stole the love as big as the Big Bang and gave nothing in return. He took everything, without returning anything.

The ship was ploughing the waves of the Baltic Sea. The waves were strong and dark, but the steel that the boat was made of was stronger. Joni was standing on the open deck, breathing in the smell of the sea and feeling the droplets of salty water on his face. He came on this cruise alone. The Turku – Stockholm – Turku route, non-stop. Around him were summer people, some of them drunk, some sober and others somewhere in between. The girls were wearing colourful dresses, which were leaping like upside down flags. The ship was sailing by the tiny islands which were showing up and disappearing in blinks of window lights. Some of the islands had beautiful houses and wooden saunas. The ship was rushing on only to come back, it did not stop.

Joni went for a drink. He drank slowly and watched others drink quickly. There was a troubadour at the bar playing on an acoustic guitar the same songs he would play repeat the next night. Joni went to the disco, even though he did not like disco music. There, he was surprised.

They played Finnish tango in the disco, and in front of the musicians on the dance floor, a man and a girl were dancing. The music was fast, the audience was clapping to the rhythm, and above it the sound of a violin lingered. The girl was looking into the man's eyes; Joni was looking at the girl. He was not looking into her eyes. He was looking at her body and her smile. You could see under the lights that her cheeks were red. Her mother had the same red cheeks. Joni knew the girl on the stage; her name was Inka. The summer was hot and the door of the disco was open. The sky was decorated with stars and a single airplane, much faster than the ship.

She saw him from the stage and gave him a smile. Joni wondered if his famous friend would come down to him, which Inka did after her performance.

-It's nice to see you. Who are you with?

-Nice to see you too! You dance wonderfully. I'm alone.

She asked for his berth number because she was often hunted by drunken journalists. He gave her the number of his berth which was located on the seventh floor.

-My berth is small.

-But without drunk journalists. They keep banging on my door.

-You are right, come. I'll buy us popcorn.

My berth has a window. We can watch the islands go by.

-Just like we used to watch the lake from the woods, when we were kids.

-See you in half an hour.

Inka went away. The drunken journalists swarmed around her and followed her every step. She was smiling, and with her mother's red cheeks she was beautiful like a flower.

Joni passed the bar, the acoustic guitar, and the hand that was strumming the strings. He bought popcorn and headed towards his berth. While he was going down to the seventh floor of the ship, he climbed onto a handrail and slowly walked along its thin wood in the empty corridor. Towards the disco he saw boys who were looking at each other's muscles and tattoos. The summer boys. He put the popcorn next to the round window of his berth. When they were children, Inka and Joni ate popcorn. They say that tattoos can be removed, but sometimes they appear again; they simply pop back up. Inka appeared in the berth and leaned next to the window, smiling and happy. Happy happy. She looked at the stars and thought how the universe is alive.

The Eyes

Joni and Inka had lived together for half a year already, in the centre of Tampere. Everything was nearby, the schools and shops, theatres and concert venues. The lakes, which surround the city, had been frozen for a long time and the snow was falling on the roofs of buildings and below them. People were dressed warmly and snow was on their hats. Joni and Inka were dancing. Everybody looked at Inka, but only the brave ones asked her for a dance. Joni looked at her, but he did not look at her body or smile. He looked at her eyes, trying to see if her eyes were looking at others.

During the next performance he followed her eyes again. Next morning he read the tabloids and what they were writing about them, about her. In the evening, drunken journalists surrounded her; sober journalists asked him a question or two, but about her. Joni was thinking of doing something brave, something which would allow him to fall. He thought that it would be a good way to get on the front pages of important newspapers.

Every night was followed by a difficult morning. They had breakfast.

Tabloids are always ugly, no matter whether they are new or old. The colours are garish and aggressive. Joni looked at a photograph of Inka in the cheap papers. Inka told him that she was leaving.

-I'm leaving.

Joni had colourful food for breakfast – red and green peppers, and white yoghurt, violet berries, red strawberries.

He heard the door open and close. It sounded like it was saying a greeting to itself while she was leaving.

But this is not a story about small people of small ambition and small love; this is not a story about Joni. This is a story about a broken-hearted man, who carries a love as powerful as the Big Bang. To hear it, we need to go to a warm place where such stories are told.

Part I

The Broken-hearted Man

1

Welcome!

I am glad you came, I am really glad.

Year after year, two years. Year after year, four years. Four times four is sixteen. It has been sixteen billion years since the Big Bang, since the cosmic fires started spreading dust, and the whole world was created out of star dust. One hundred and ten elements make up the universe, You, and me. The movement of the Big Band created time and space.

Now you are standing in front of me, paying for your sauna entrance fee and looking into my eyes.

You expect me to tell you a story, my story – the story of a broken-hearted man.

Alright. But you are not allowed to change it.

I am going to tell you a story about longing, about a Serbian immigrant, about a famous Finnish dancer, about an infamous acrobat, about friends and musicians from Lapland and about a Cambodian girl, fearless like a penguin, who connected them all. I know, when you think of a penguin you think of something funny, even cute, but definitely not fearless; this is why I used that word – fearless – because penguins, in fact, know no fear.

I am going to tell you a story about love so sad, as beautiful as tango and as strong as the restlessness of the Big Bang. Yes, that strong. The one hundred and ten elements and my longing start in a place that would seem like nowhere to You, but that nowhere was the whole world; a sauna, next to a lake and woods, near a small village. The story begins apparently uneventfully, or at least that's what it felt like, but in fact it starts with a restless friendship full of love.

I am glad you came, let's go:

2
Cyclicality

Sauna

Panu is the central figure of our story.

Panu thought that all events were cyclical, just like everything in nature, just like everything about planets. Panu never left his village and he socialised only in the sauna, where he met his friend every day. Outside of the sauna he did not socialise. He often thought about his happy childhood. He thought that the cyclicality of nature would return his happiness.

In his childhood Panu had loved, a beautiful girl named Inka, who later on was in a relationship with his friend. Panu was right when he thought that there was cyclicality, but he shouldn't have hoped that nature would return what he never had.

Our past is uncertain and we build it consciously in our minds. Panu got one kiss from Inka and out of that kiss he built the certainty of her return to his embrace. The funny, pathetic Panu.

-Nothing ever happens here. – Aleksi said.

-I should not be upset about my life being stupid, because I am not doing anything smart. –, thought Panu.

The sky was suspended over the lake and the sauna, like a blue cloudless dome. Aleksi was looking at the frozen nature through the window. He was not alone. The heat of the water that turned to steam moments ago hit his back. His gaze was outside, and his friend, Panu, just next to him. Panu was smiling; he was entertained looking at Aleksi's gaze lost in the distance. It seemed to him that Aleksi's feelings were covered in snow, just like his surroundings. Aleksi was looking at the blue sky; there was nothing in it. The tree tops, tucked under the snow were looking at the white dust dissolve with the swipe of the wind. In summertimes, when they were children, they used to play among those trees in the forest by the sauna. They picked wild blueberries and strawberries and gave them to their friends, Inka and Anna. Aleksi remembered how they made shacks from branches with his friend Joni. He could see his smile. He remembered his childlike gaze. Anna and Inka ave him a hug for each strawberry he gave them. He was happy, wearing a smile on his ruddy cheeks.

Now, older and heavier he looked into the distance and spoke with a deep voice:

-Nothing ever happens around here.

Panu took a small wooden ladle and started pouring water onto the hot sauna stones, transforming into steam.

The heat was climbing from the stove up along the walls of the sauna towards the wooden ceiling. Aleksi leaned forward and covered his burning ears. He wanted to see what the temperature was but the heat of the steam prevented him from doing so. Panu spread his arms, like a victorious boxer, and waited for the hot air with a smile on his face. Then he stood up to get even more heat and stayed like that for a few minutes, after which he went outside. He stepped into the cold snow with his bare feet, while steam emanated from his body. He went to the lake, entered the cold water, swam a few strokes and came out. He sat on a wooden bench and stared at the dome of the sky.

-Panu, take this. –, Aleksi brought a can of beer.

Aleksi was wet, having just gotten out of water.

They were looking up at the blue dome and sensed the height of the sky. They took in deep breaths, while their bodies slowly lost heat. The lake, the forest and they were all becoming one. When the cold air started to feel unpleasant, they returned to the sauna.

3

Come with me, please hold those logs for me, I need to put them into the stove. Thank you.

Look at how it burns. Fire! We Finns, we believe that fire came from the sky. Beautiful.

You see, in 2013, a long time ago, the internet made encounters between people even stranger. internet was used everywhere: in Finland, in Serbia, in Cambodia… and, just like every other good tool, it was used both for wonderful and horrible things. I am telling you this, because soon a Serbian and Cambodian immigrant will meet in Finland, and I do not know if that is a wonderful thing, but it definitely is interesting if we think about the sheer probability of it.

A Cambodian woman connects this story, a lovely little woman. She was here yesterday.

How many Cambodians do you know? I know her and I've seen many southeast Asians here in the sauna; they come on Thursdays, I don't know why. I don't ask them where they come from, I'm too shy. Imagine if I said to them – Here is your entrance, and where do you come from? – It's really not appropriate. And they all look the same to me, no matter what country they come from: Laos, Thailand, Cambodia, Vietnam… they all smile in a similar way. I think they might come here to study, I'm not sure. And where do *you* come from? Forgive my question, it does not matter, you don't have to answer. Your origin has nothing to do with this story; we are talking about the broken-hearted man here, about Panu and his longing and his never-fulfilled wish, Inka.

-How many funambulists do you know?

I know one funambulist, a person that walks on a tightrope. Yes, they are very rare. Soon you will get to know him too. Soon you will get to know the Cambodian woman and the Serbian immigrant; alas, his level of education is unforgivably low, but let's see what the reason for it is:

4
Non-existence

Tampere

The cyclicality of nature was bringing to Panu and Aleksi an uncertain past in the form of two funny immigrants. They did not even know one of them.

It was ten degrees below zero and snowing outside. Inside the dance hall, which was heated with big old radiators, the floor, the people, the walls and tables were covered with the yellow spots of light from the disco ball. The spots were moving fast, much faster than the rhythm of Finnish tango. Dressed like an elderly gentleman in an old suit and hat, although only in his thirties, Joni was leaning against the wall next to the entrance and said:

-There is only one Elvis, but there is also only one Olavi Virta.

The Serbian immigrant did not know what Elvis had to do with Finnish Tango, so he thought that Joni was comparing the greatness of the two singers. He had no idea who Olavi was, so he asked Joni, not knowing that his question would provoke an unexpected reaction:

-Who is Olavi?

Around them couples were waddling like gigantic birds, Joni was looking at them for some time only to reply with a conclusion full of disbelief:

-You don't know who Olavi Virta is. You don't know who Olavi is.

The Serbian immigrant knew Inka, he knew her personally and he saw her dance. To Joni's disappointment, he didn't know who Olavi was.

-Tango is the dance of complete surrender to feelings, a dance where concentration and complete relaxation are merged into one. Olavi is the Finnish king of sad thoughts. When he sings, his voice carries sadness mixed with happiness; sadness and happiness in one same song.

Maybe I am ignorant, thought the Serbian immigrant, but it seems that I am also very ugly. Women were approaching Joni, not the immigrant. A girl in a long red dress approached Joni and took him to dance. The immigrant was left alone in the sea of decorative spots from the disco ball that were running towards him and from him. He sat down and looked around at the crowd which was dancing in a circle. Joni is a funambulist, a tightrope walker, and you could tell that from the way he danced. The man who was standing above the abyss of destiny every day had a harmonious dancing trot, so harmonious that every woman who danced with him looked beautiful. The immigrant sat through the entire evening, enjoying the view of the ladies in other men's embraces, only to hear from Joni at the end of the evening that Inka was the best.

Inka! Blonde, sweet, smiling, the best. When she danced the whole of Finland admired. Argentina, Serbia, France admired. When she danced she owned the festivals. She never provoked envy; she only showed how beautiful this world was.

And then suddenly, something happened; Inka isolated herself from everybody here, for months; she disappeared into nowhere.

16

The Serbian immigrant went towards home, peeking into the window of a record store under the cold light of the city lamps on the high street along the way. When he arrived, he closed the door and left it unlocked. He jumped into a hot shower and was at peace under the relaxing waterfall when he heard a bang and realised that it was the door.

He got out of the shower and saw a young, beautiful Asian woman in a wet red top and black panties.

-What are you doing here? – he asked her with fear.

She looked him in the eyes. It was obvious that she was agitated, that she had just run away and had found herself at his place. She did not reply.

She was almost naked; he took his bathrobe and wrapped it around her. She was petite and beautiful, like a little girl.

He was naked; he took a towel and wrapped it around his hips.

He thought of kicking her out, but she would die in the cold outside. He thought of many things, and one of the possibilities was to let her stay in the apartment. She did not say why she came into his world. The scared immigrant gave her his long t-shirt, which made for a night gown on her small body, and he converted the sofa into a bed. He asked her if she was hungry, but she wasn't. The city lights were blinking under the window of his one-bedroom apartment. He did not roll down the blinds; he preferred looking at life coloured by neon. He looked at her large slanted eyes with fear; they were good and warm. The snowflakes were falling on the other side of the glass. He lay on the bed near the sofa. He thought of the high clouds that the snow was falling from. He thought of the fresh air and the power and gentleness of nature. He looked at the beautiful girl in front of him, and was full of fear. It seemed that she was crying silently. He did not know how to comfort her. He did not even know what to say to her. Suddenly she gave him a smile; he saw it thanks to the blue neon light. He replied with a scared look when she interrupted the snowflake-decorated silence with a voice:

-They are near! They are just next to us!

5
Hot Bodies

The train

The train was rushing through the birch forest
Through the silent slopes of light towards the low
sun
The branches, the trunks, the frozen snow
Underneath a blue sky without birds
And the lake, the watery mirror of the sky
Blonde girls are running towards the lake
Naked and smiling
Towards the frozen mirror
Towards the opening where they will cool their hot
bodies
On the other side of my glass wall

As you can see, Panu is wonderful. At least to me, I prefer the errors of passion to the indifference of intellectualism. But let's return to our immigrants. The cosmic fires carry many energies, electricity being among them. Men figured out how to connect interests through electricity via the internet, which is good and bad, but let's talk about the good things. The internet helped tango spread all over the world. You are right; the fast spread of tango is due to its motifs, because sadness, love and beauty are seeded everywhere across our little planet, and the fearless Cambodian girl was, before coming to Finland, a modest mistress of tango. Inspired by the beauty of sadness and the harmony of Inka's dance, she fell in love with the melancholy that is embodied in the dance.

Inka was everywhere, like mysterious beauty, like Panu's longing, like a distant image.

Inka, do you remember? I still keep the newspaper articles with her photos. Look at this picture; look at what came from the dust of the Big Bang – gentleness, sophistication, smiles. It does not matter that the newspaper has turned yellow, look at this picture. I am not surprised that Panu fell so much in love with Inka. She broke his heart, even though she did not mean to do it; she was not even aware that she had done it. She gave him a piece of a happy childhood in the sauna and in the forest next to it, many happy days of youth and a kiss when she was leaving to study to in Rovaniemi. Afterwards, Inka became interested in dance, then tango, and then she left for Tampere where she reached the news, newspapers, internet, festivals and other people's hearts.

Panu started collecting newspapers with her pictures and going to the sauna every day, hoping that Inka would grow tired and return to the place where she gave him the goodbye kiss. Panu became a blockhead, the fool with a good and broken heart, who spent his days in the sauna, where at the time of this story, he was with his friend Aleksi to share the present and the hopes that the past will return and ask for salvation.

Yes, this is the story of his sad love, beautiful like tango and strong as the restlessness of the Big Bang.

Let's return to the friends who meet in the sauna.

The Fruitlessness of Effort

Sauna

Panu could not explain to himself why he never left his village. He was afraid of change, but he did not know why. Maybe the immobility of conformity, maybe the control of his uncertain past, or the belief in cyclicality and the fear that leaving would disturb everything that was his life.

-Nothing ever happens here? Nothing ever happens here?,- Panu was saying to Aleksi, but Aleksi was quiet, bearing the heat that was coming in waves.

-And what is Joni doing?-, Panu uttered the question about the once dear friend.

-Joni is teaching people balance; he is teaching them how to walk the tightrope and fences, without falling.

Panu nodded and took the wooden ladle. He threw water four times.

At that very moment an Elvis Presley impersonator appeared in the door. He was wearing an enormous wig that looked like a caricature of Elvis's haircut. He said – Good day – and sat opposite Aleksi. Panu moved away from the stove and sat next to the fake Elvis.

-So, Mister Elvis, from where are you coming to our parts?-, asked Aleksi.

-From Spain. I am going to an Elvis impersonator festival just near here.

-You don't have a Spanish accent when you speak English. Actually, you sound American.–, Aleksi noticed.

-You are right, I am American by birth. I studied singing in America. I was a tenor. My aunt had already lived in Spain when I finished my studies. Tenors are in great demand in Spain, so I married my aunt to get Spanish papers. Nobody checks blood liaisons there, so that is how I became a Spaniard.

-Nice.–, Panu said and added: -Hola amigo.

-Hola amigo.–, the Spanish-American answered.

-What made you become an Elvis impersonator?–, Panu asked indiscreetly.

Outside, the wind played with the tiny snowflakes that it stole from the trees. Aleksi was looking out of the window and wanted to feel the winter. He went out and took the cold snow and started rubbing it over his steaming body. The snow was melting on his skin. The cold air was entering his lungs, the sky was flying like a big breath. He returned to the sauna and heard the Spanish-American say:

-One clear thought has tortured me for years – the fruitlessness of effort!

-The fruitlessness of effort?-, Panu was confused.

-Yes, the fruitlessness of the effort of all of us who want to learn how to sing. I understood that nobody will be able reach Elvis's grandiosity. That is why I decided to try to live and look like him. I wanted to become him. That is the only way for me to become whole!

-What about Placido Domingo? – Aleksi asked, not knowing that you don't ask an Elvis impersonator questions of comparison and relativity.

-What *about* Placido Domingo? When Elvis starts with "It's now or never", when his voice resonates, even the birds start crying. The *birds* start crying!

And, as if he was one of those birds himself, the fake Elvis started crying, and then he let his voice out to resonate loudly all over the sauna in the form of the "It's Now or Never" song, resembling the real Elvis.

Panu poured more water over the lava stones. The heat became hotter, its waves hitting the faces of the surprised Finns and the face of the crying, singing American who married his own aunt to be able to sing in Spain and to arrive via the conjured wonder of the Lappish sauna.

8

Immigration is desperation; immigrants do all kinds of abnormal things to be able to live normally, even marry their own aunts. But those immigrants who have not settled at the place where they arrived, lie to themselves and others that they have settled, just like our funny Serbian immigrant.

You see, it's not nice for me to say it while the person is crying, but I hate the fake Elvis. You will get to know who he is later, and why he appeared at the sauna.

Come over. Open the door for me, the stove door, so that I can put some wood.

Aleksi, disappointed, was sitting every day for several hours in the sauna, with friendly comfort from Panu because of his seemingly failed Cambodian relationship. Inka, the love that the other man never overcame, that is Panu's love, will come back soon. Inka ran away because of her relationship with Joni; I think that she became pregnant by him. I am not sure, but the child, who was here yesterday, looks like Joni; a pretty little girl.

Ever since he disappeared, Joni never came back; I will tell you about it soon. I had asked you how many funambulists you knew, but now I realise that the right question would be: How many people who are prone to falling do you know? Probably many. You see, Joni is one of them, very charming and skilled in his walk, but obsessed with falling down the precipice beneath the tightrope of life.

Panu and Joni used to be best friends when they were young. They were in love with the same woman. Joni was more successful, although never devoted to anybody, except to himself and to the fascination of his own falling. Panu stayed in the village, in love with Inka, forever.

Please hold the door of the stove. Take the handle, but be careful, it's hot. Wait for me to put some more wood inside. Can you smell it? You know, I love my job – to work in the sauna is like being an invisible doctor for the heart and soul. It is nice to know that you make others feel good.

But, let's return to our story and the unusual meeting of the Cambodian woman and the Serb.

9
Botum, the Woman from the Net

Tampere

-Who is near?

-My kidnappers.

The night, lit with blue neon, was bringing sleep to the slow-passing minutes. The bed and the sofa were swimming in the blue light. The Serbian immigrant was scared, but he was also glad to have a guest in the form of a petite, beautiful woman. Big snowflakes were coming to the window to hear what the guest was asking him.

-Are you sleeping?

-No. Sleep is coming slowly to me.

-Are you going to work tomorrow morning?

-I am. Biology. Important experiments.-, he answered.

-Can I stay tomorrow too?-, she asked.

-Sure. You can stay. Who are you?

-I am Botum, a woman from the net.

He had never heard such a name. It sounded beautiful. He thought about her name while the drowsiness was bringing him the image of a big net that caught his guest. He was watching her try to find the exit from the net without an exit. The net was made for small women and it was covering the entire world. In his dream he saw Botum become a child who turns into a golden bird and then flies across the world to his apartment. He had a feeling that she came here because of him, not because of herself.

As if she knew about this dream, she said, through the blueness of the neon light:

-Can I ask you something?

-Go ahead.

-Can I use your phone? I want to tell my mother to go somewhere safe.

-Call her from my computer; I don't have a phone. Also, that way nobody can locate the number, because it is not defined on the computer.

He stood up and walked across the sea of neon blue, took a beer from the fridge and sat down watching the petite beautiful Cambodian girl make a call from the computer. She was talking quietly, with a smile on her face. The pain and the beauty of nature were in front of him, the strength and the gentleness, the horror and love. The snowflakes were hitting the window; snowflakes don't worry, they have no heart. He went outside to the small balcony of his apartment. The snow was falling on the blue neon, highlighting the letters "Private Massage", letters he did not notice before.

He returned and lowered the blind. He sat looking at the woman who ran away to him to find freedom.

-I came as a woman from the net. I was supposed to marry a man I met on the net, but when I arrived to Finland, some people met me, put me in a van, took my passport and said that they would kill my family and me if I tried to escape. They put me in an apartment in the building next door among the so called masseuses.

-Why don't you go to the police?–, he asked.

-They told me that going to the police would be fatal.

-Who told you that?

-The other women.

-Why?–, he asked, surprised.

-They said that our kidnappers have connections there.

-Who were you supposed to marry? Did you see his photo on the net?

-Yes, I saw him. We talked many times. His name is Aleksi and he lives in a village in Lapland. He studied Spanish here in Tampere.At least that's what he told me. Now I start to think that he was part of this scheme.

-Maybe your Aleksi does not exist. Maybe he was just an actor.

-I don't know what to believe.

In the dark apartment a thick line was standing; the wide blue light under the blind and big snowflakes. The light was beautiful like the sea and clear skies. The light was dirty like sick desire.

Botum started sobbing and sounded like a small girl. She covered herself with a blanket. He asked her again if she was hungry, but she did not speak anymore.

He hoped that she had fallen asleep when silence replaced the sobbing.

10
Do You Remember, Mielikki

The train

Through the branches and leaves
Nobody stops to see you
Are we waiting for life without trees
Are we going to make oxygen with machines and robots
Through the branches and leaves we hunted beasts
Do you remember, Mielikki
Through the branches and leaves our people were passing
Through the branches and leaves we were afraid of bears
You protected our herds, Mielikki
You brought us luck
You healed our reindeer

The cosmic fires are carrying our planet with the force of creation and destruction. Fascinating! But on our extraordinary planet there are terribly bad people who trade in human lives. How many times have you passed by a place where there are women slaves? Yes, we do it every day. I believe, as I always have, that love is stronger than human trafficking, which was proven by our little fearless Cambodian woman. I don't believe her kidnappers to be so evil, because they were very dumb. Supreme evil requires supreme intelligence, but love still beats it.

Love was also in the sauna where friends were getting together. Panu often comforted Aleksi, although he himself needed comfort. Broken-hearted, he did not leave his village; he was invoking his childhood and longed for Inka. In the sauna, Panu felt better. The heat of the sauna relaxes the muscles, improves blood circulation and the release of endorphin. Endorphins are the chemicals that tell our body and soul to feel well. Among other things, it is because of endorphins that Panu was saying that sauna was a sacred place. The cosmos is endlessly large, but still there are only a few places that lead the chemistry of our body to pleasure.

In the context of space and probability, the uniqueness of sauna is extraordinary. I knew a band in Lapland that had gigs in saunas; they played sauna-punk music. While the planet is whipping through space, while the cosmos is rushing endlessly in its growth, they were playing in these small wooden spaces. Endorphins, music, sauna and beer. The cosmic fires carry our planet, while Panu and Aleksi are sitting in the land of eternal snow. Our planet is fascinating, just like Panu's longing.

In the context of fascination and its opposite, let's mention the musicians, they deserve it although I hate one of them; they are important for our story.

12

Musicians at a Railway Station on the Blue Horizon
Popularity

The musicians were sitting inside a warm railway station. Two of them were angry at themselves; the third one was quiet and calm.

-It would be great if we were popular.

-And why is that?-, the quiet one asked.

-More people would hear our music. We would be able to share our ideas, our love with others.

-Yes, but...

-But what?

-We would have to compromise. They would tell us to make songs for thirteen-year-old girls and seventeen-year-old boys.-, the quiet one said.

-Why for them?

-Because they buy the most.-, the quiet one said.

-A small compromise is not bad.

-A small compromise is very bad.

-But the money. The money is lovely!

-But the music that makes the money is too often not lovely.-, the quiet one said.

By the way, I hate the quiet one, it should be noted.

13
50%, 100%

Sauna

Under the cloudless blue dome, next to the frozen lake, in the frozen forest the sauna was echoing with the warm tenor that was singing "It's Now or Never". Panu thought that life was more imaginative than our personal imaginations, and that it offers us situations that we don't expect. The surprise was making his smile wide, his lungs full of warm air and pleasure. He listened to the entire performance of the fake Elvis and then went out and with a fast pace went to the hole in the ice. He swam, returned and sat down. He took a beer and felt the joyful beating rhythm of his heart. The forest, although frozen, looked intimately familiar; he played in it when he was a child. It was a place of discovery and smiles. Under his feet the hard snow began to melt. His breaths were taking in the entirety of nature. He was losing himself in the view and then he sensed the height of the sky, as pleasant as the cold air in the lungs. In the distance he discerned two silhouettes.

He drank up the beer, returned, looked at this friend and said:

-Aleksi, is it really true that nothing ever happens? Look – we even have Elvis, and not just any Elvis, but a *weeping* Elvis.

Aleksi did not comment on that observation

of Panu's. He was looking at the tearful man who was not singing anymore.

-I've never left this village. You know that Aleksi, don't you?

-I know, Panu.

-And do you know that Inka is back?

-I know.

-I think she returned because of me! Women go crazy after they meet me, and the madness becomes incurable. That's why they come back, to be near me.–, Panu answered and at the same time wished that his joke were true.

-You first have to be smart to be able to lose your mind.–, Aleksi praised and scolded Panu, who liked this comment.

-Out of two girls from our village, one came back.–, Panu said.

-Out of two girls from our village, one came back.–, Aleksi confirmed.

Panu was smiling. He approached the stove and slowly poured water over the hot stones. He was doing it with surprising caution. Childhood was coming back in the form of gorgeous Inka; the many life surprises were giving Panu a sense of fulfilment. The heat was climbing up the walls towards the corners. The whole body relaxes in the heat of the sauna. It is beautiful to be alive, it is beautiful to have a body, it is beautiful to be in the sauna, Panu thought.

-Yes, that's 50%.–, Aleksi went back to his conclusion about the return, not knowing that Anna had also returned and that the number had secretly increased to one hundred percent.

-Maybe Inka even comes to the sauna.

-Have you seen her?

-No. They say she's lost weight. They say she is not going out at all.

Aleksi approached the stove and slowly poured ladle after ladle, ten times. The hot steam was transforming the existence into unbearableness. The weeping Spanish-American stopped crying; he lowered his head between his hands, covering his ears. He managed to stay a good half minute and then ran out. As he was leaving, two musicians who were standing outside the door ran away together with him.

Through the window, in the distance, you could see a train gliding quickly past on the cold sticky rails; you could not see it often. And suddenly, the window view changed into the face of a moose; the big creature looked into the steamy, naked, hot world that was filling with life-changing hope.

The creature looked at the two, then turned to the forest and pranced back, disappearing between the tree trunks.

-Freedom is our responsibility; that is why we created rules and laws.-, how jokingly Panu was saying this.

But some things were getting out of control. The cosmic fires carry our planet. I read somewhere that in that long-ago 2013, the planet had 29.8 million slaves, or people who were owned by somebody against their own will. It is a large number! But there is one thing that is protecting Finland from evil, ever since the Viking times: Surma, a horrible sudden death, black and cruel. Some say that Surma looks like a big black dog with a tail in the shape of a snake, but I believe it is something completely different.

I believe that a man who wants to live here has to be a man of good will, and with good will he has to adapt to the society If he does not adapt, Surma will find him. The forest always gave us enormous wealth, but the Vikings knew that only with good will can you find riches, only with good will and only together with the forest-dwelling people, not against them, not despite them.

In this story you will find out how Surma ended with the kidnappers who were looking for Botum in Lapland. The evil people wanted to use other people's love, only to end up near the broken-hearted man. Yes, near Panu, they ended up lifeless, like frozen mammoths.

Let's go back to our funny immigrants and their serious loves. Let's find out how they are adapting.

15

Bios Logos

Morning came and the Serbian immigrant got ready for work. He worked in a warehouse, where he carried heavy boxes in and out. The job did not sound inspiring or prestigious, so he never told anyone what he was actually doing. Although he had to suffer hardship, at least others did not have to worry about him. On the job he liked working with people in the warehouse. There is something special in the cargo handover; maybe it is empathy mixed with relief. Anyhow, whatever the reason for his pathology, he lied pathologically that he worked as a biologist on important experiments. He graduated with a degree in Biology, so, at least theoretically, he was a biologist.

His guest was asleep, a big girl on a small sofa.

He woke the Cambodian girl up and told her that he would see her in the afternoon.

-Where are you going?-, she asked him sleepily.

-I'm going to work.-, he replied, full of desire to tell the truth, and added: -I work as a biologist on important experiments.

-Do you know that my kidnappers are in the building next door? Just on the other side of this wall.

-They live in the centre just like us.-, he replied jokingly scared and added: -Don't go to the balcony.

-Come back soon.

-You have nothing to be afraid of. Also, when somebody drops newspapers through that slot in the door, don't get scared. It's normal here.

-I can't believe it. They drop the newspapers through a slot in the door.

-They do. It's usually just advertisements.

-Okay, good to know. I'll wait for you.

-Do you have a plan? What are you going to do afterwards?-, he asked.

-I don't have a plan, I don't have a passport, I can't even go to the police.-, she replied.

-Get some rest. We'll think of something later.

Then he went out and left the small apartment full of scattered books and CDs. He rode on a bus that went through a thick birch forest.

The forest was especially beautiful; he realised that the trees, which grew from tossed seeds, had complete symmetry, and that the Sun was spreading its rays behind the trunks, just like cities spread their streets. He was looking at the forest and thought about the morality of creation and the change of the world. He thought about love songs, about light, about shadows and about semi-round city gates.

He was the first to arrive at work; he arranged some boxes to resemble streets that crossed at city squares. He imagined market places next to universities, cafes near theatres, when his boss arrived and with a surprised yet gentle voice said:

-You are fired.

He stood and waited for a reply. He expected some kind of reaction, a response, emotion. His boss was a good and hard-working man, and firing the funny immigrant proved that the boss was also reasonable and just.

The immigrant was watching the boxes that carried merchandise. Out of them he created a new meaning, neglecting their primary purpose. The streets were not carrying the names of Neda Arnerić, nor Jefimija, nor Mihajlo Pupin, nor Nikola Tesla, nor Milutin Milanković, nor were the squares named after Monika Seleš, or Mileva Marić, or Mihailo Petrović Alas, or Andrić, or Crnjanski; all of the streets and squares were named after the friends he had not seen in a long time.

The cardboard city that he had just created will be left without a mayor. He was not sorry that he got fired; it had been a long time that he felt like he needed a change. The change materialised in the form of a cardboard Renaissance.

16
Another World

The train

A group of young people sat in front of my seat
They left their skis on the floor and on the metal
rails above
Youth and sport together, the beauty of smiles
Next to them, on the other side of the glass wall
The forest was interrupted with spaces covered with
snow
The whiteness was decorated with the train lights
The group of young people hugged and looked
through the window
The train was diving into green northern lights
The Sami people believe that northern lights are
made out of ancestors' souls
I was travelling across other souls

Would you like a shot of vodka? I have one sometimes, it warms you up nicely. Beer started to make me tired, it's the age. Look at the people who just got out of the lake, look how they are sitting, outside of everything, a closed circle, longing and belonging together, strength and tenderness together, hot and cold. That is sauna.

The cosmic fires, You and me. Our stories, our lives. Our sorrow, our love, our happiness, our story. Let's go back to our story. Panu was happy that his love was back, and excited about the upcoming encounter. He wondered if Inka would remember the goodbye kiss and if she would give him another one, then give herself to him.

After all this time, I now understand that our Finns were emotionally weak; Panu in his complete commitment, Aleksi in his pursuit of love electronically, comfortably protected with distance. Commitment and humility. On the other hand, out of that emotional weakness all of the poetry of this world is built. The sublimity of feeling is in humility.

And look at our immigrants; I am speechless. They are simply immature. I'll talk about them later; I have to tell you about the musicians, so that you can connect what actually happened.

18
Musicians at a Railway Station on the Blue Horizon
Decision

The musicians were sitting inside a warm train station. Two of them were angry at themselves; the third one was quiet and calm. They had been playing for years in saunas and arctic festivals. The quiet and calm musician loved the midnight sun and the music they were creating, he knew that they had the melody and the story, he knew that the other two were angry at themselves because neither of them was a singer.

-We don't need a good singer! He doesn't have to hit all the notes; he has to carry the song, feel it, to make us feel it, make others feel it.

-You're right, we know it, but we cannot find a singer that would fit in our story.

-Maybe I am the one?–, the calm one asked calmly. –The two of you are so loud that I never come to the fore. You play excellently, but you can't sing, so you can try me if you want-, said the calm one calmly.

-You? Don't be ridiculous! You chirp like a bird.

-Actually, I am a tenor.-, the calm one said.

-You, a tenor. How come we get to know about this only now?

-You two are much louder. Also, I studied singing.

-So go ahead, prove it.

-If I only sang to you two, you'll say it's not

good enough.–, the calm one said.

-That's true. We'll keep underestimating you. It's called friendship.

-Or friends' unfriendliness.

-Whatever. Go sing to the two guys in the sauna. If you convince them that you can sing like Elvis, you will become our singer.

-Why Elvis?

-You lived in America, and I have an Elvis wig here. An Elvis impersonator gave it to me when he participated in a nearby festival.

-Okay. I'll go to them. I'll wear the wig.–, the quiet one said.

-And to make your task a bit harder, you should tell them that you come from Spain!

-I can't speak Spanish, but okay! You can look through the window and listen to what is happening inside.

-Deal. If you succeed, then you are our new singer.

- Okay. Let me say a prayer first, and I'm on my way:

Oh thank you, God, that I live here, where there is sound. Imagine if I lived somewhere else in the universe, somewhere where you cannot hear sounds.

I am thankful because my ears can hear the music of Africa, Europe, Asia and the rest of the world.

Oh thank you, God, that my hands play instruments. I get lost in music when my fingers are dancing.

Thank you that I have a heart. Because my heart feels joy, my heart feels sorrow.

My thoughts are full of music, just like Tuscany is full of beautiful buildings.

My music comes from everywhere, from the

whole world.

Thank you.

It is not okay for me to say this, particularly after this man's prayer, but I hate this quiet musician. It will be clear to you why.

Let's go back to the friends who were meeting in the sauna.

19
The Grown-Up People

Sauna

-I am not trying to become a better person; I am just trying to feel better. – Panu thought.

-Nothing ever happens here! – Aleksi said as he was pouring water over the hot stones.

The water was slowly falling onto the stove. It was flowing over the hot lava pebbles being converted into a semi-visible steam. The heat was increasing with the moisture; it was climbing up the wooden walls and hitting the naked backs of people. They were sitting without moving, suffering the wave of heat, their ears were scorched, but their faces were carrying calmness. In the sauna and outside of it, no matter how much it burns, you never show your pain to others. The heat goes to the corners, to the other side of the stove. Pain is a personal thing, and whining is embarrassing. Stamina and pride were sitting quietly and the hot evaporated water was stinging. During those moments, there is something ancient called beer. Every sip seems like travelling to eternity. And then the challenge is born, the expansion of boundaries. Panu went to the corner, because it is the hottest spot.

-How nice it was when we were kids!–, Panu said, touching his feet and realising that they were too cold.

-How come?-, Aleksi asked.

-We played so nicely! The five of us!-, Panu answered, raising his feet to the ceiling of the sauna.

-We did! Joni, you, Anna, Inka and me. Next to the lake, in the colourful house with toys.-, Aleksi answered looking at Panu attempting to stand at a right angle, upside down, with his feet on the ceiling, and poured some more water on the hot sauna stones.

-So, what happened to us?-, the upside-down Panu asked.

The sauna became quiet. It contained two friends on a flat surface of the planet covered with a blue dome. Panu could feel that his feet were getting warm fast, and he banged his toes on the ceiling. He was happy to have his friend next to him, an interlocutor in this hot refuge. The sun was sending its low rays, looking like the work a lighting technician who is beaming the strong lights from a corner, through a foggy sauna window.

-We grew up! We became adults.-, Aleksi answered.

-I never imagined grown up people would be like this.

Aleksi glanced at the upside-down Panu, and asked him if he would like a beer, then went to fetch two cans without waiting for the answer.

Although they were not adding more water to the lava stones, the sauna became steamy. Both were surprised, it seemed as if the sauna became alive.

-Sauna is a holy place! Sauna is alive!-, the upside-down Panu said.

-Please, tell me why sauna is holier than a living room?-, Aleksi asked.

Panu was not answering. The sauna was pleasantly hot, although full of moisture. The friends in the sauna did not know that the change was an omen that foretold the arrival of an important guest.

Navigation satellites float above the thin atmosphere, sending signals, reporting, sometimes – luckily - incorrectly. One hundred and ten elements make this world, You, the cosmic fires, me, our funny immigrants and their funny ambitions. The Serb fell for Anna. I have known Anna for a long time, and she was here yesterday with her lively, smiling children. Anna is very beautiful for sure, but it is her joy that is attractive, which seems to work on funny immigrants. Our women are taken by immigrants!

I will not elaborate now on the object of Panu's beloved, Inka. I want to tell you what happened to the immigrants and the kidnappers. You see, Surma, the sudden, black death caught up with the kidnappers. It was not a death by higher destiny, the evil fate, nor was it death in the form of a big black dog with a snake tail. It was death by cell phone navigation. How come? you are asking. I will explain now.

Musicians at a Railway Station on the Blue Horizon
Cell phone navigation

The musicians were sitting in the warm railway station. Two of them were angry at themselves; the third one was quiet and calm. The angry musicians were angry because of their jealousy. It was hard for them to accept that the quiet musician sang better than both of them and that they will not be able to croak in saunas, only play their instruments and be quiet. But the most painful thing was that, when they would sing, it would have to be quietly, like some sorry background voices.

The situation at the railway station was tensely quiet.

The quiet musician was looking at his cell phone and the navigation application in it, trying to find the railway station and set it as a starting point, and the sauna on the other side of the lake as the destination. He noticed that something was wrong and that the navigation satellites were very incorrect at the Arctic Circle.

He heard a car pull over at the station, its engine screeching in the cold.

At that moment, resembling bewildered monsters dressed in big beasts' furs, the stupid kidnappers appeared, in search of Botum, or at least Aleksi. They were carrying weapons, fur hats and inadequate boots that made their feet freeze.

-We are looking for Botum!–, one of the kidnappers said.

-Good for you.–, a musician answered, it

was one of the angry ones.

-We are looking for Aleksi! We know that he spends his time in a nearby sauna.-, another kidnapper said.

-Why are you looking at your phone? Who are you calling?-, the third kidnapper asked and snatched the phone from the quiet musician's hand.

-Ahaa! The elephant has come to his village! Look, here is the sauna.

-Great! Great!-, rejoiced the stupid kidnappers with their seemingly smart friend. Then they returned to the car that was still screeching in the cold.

-After 50 meters turn left.-, said the mechanised voice on the mobile phone.

And the car slowly disappeared in the direction opposite to the blue horizon into the white coldness in its futile search for the sauna, a petrol station and, in a desperate attempt to get warm, away from the cold air that was slowly squeezing them.

22
Angkor Wat

Tampere

There are holy places on this planet which people visit because of their beauty and spirituality. The funny immigrant thought of consumer products as meaningless; he wanted their large packages to bring together knowledge, spirituality and beauty. Into the middle of the square made out of hard paper, imagined actors were coming, and imagined children were playing. He was not surprised that he lost his job; he was neither efficient, nor did he like himself in the environment from which he had just been exiled, unless we count the cardboard Renaissance moment. He was thankful to his boss and his words and said:

-Thank you. It was time for a change.

-Thank you too. Goodbye.

After several years of cargo exchange and exchanging looks over the box transfers, they ended it with few words; he thanked the people who wished him luck, collected his few personal belongings and left.

In his small life, in his heart that wanted to be big, a bus station was standing. And a bus that comes from a forest where warehouses are, and leaves slowly to get lost, just like a disoriented moose among frozen tree trunks. In the centre of Tampere, a city squeezed between two frozen lakes, he bought a long red wig for his guest in a Goth fashion store.

He returned to the apartment, the rent for

which he will now not be able to afford next month. Botum was listening to smooth jazz, bathed in the window light, masked by a pair of sunglasses. Books and CDs were on the shelves. The apartment was bright, clean and radiant. She was wearing his yellow-green shirt; he was happy to see her. He hugged her, and had the feeling that he was hugging freedom. He gave her the red wig, winter boots and jacket and they went outside. Baggy and brave, small and adult, gentle, she was as strong as a mountain river. While they were heading to the blues bar on the high street, he was watching the trees decorated with LEDs, the trees silently bore their heavy weights. In the bar they listened to blues and jazz, drank beer, talked about music... A gig started; a few musicians crammed into a space smaller than 2 square meters and played songs. Happy, they spread their happiness to others, talked to the musicians, danced without rhythm, without sense, but within temporary happiness. She, with a wig and sunglasses, hidden and present; and he, simply funny.

The next day, around noon, they were breathing in the fresh air and walking through snowflakes. They were walking through a forest next to a lake and looked at the blue, red and green boats piled along the frozen lake shore. They looked at shadows and reflections. They talked about the beauty of colours and the smell of the forest, when the immigrant invited her to go for doughnuts at Pyynikin näkontörni, which is an observation tower on a wooded hill. Up there is where Anna works, he said.

-Who is Anna?

-Anna is a Finn from the far north. Anna makes the doughnuts.–, he looked at the walls of the tall tower where doughnuts were being made.

-Who is Anna?-, she repeated the question.

-Anna is the person I love. I would like to grow old with her.

-So young and you already think about growing old?-, Botum asked through a smile.

-I don't know if I am young.

They reached the tower, where he found out that Anna had left. She had left forever for the land of eternal snow!

They took a doughnut and a cup of tea each. They sat at a table, though he felt as if he was sitting in the emptiness of the universe. Botum was looking at him with a sad smile. And in his stead, she started to cry.

-It reminds me of Angor Wat, where I was supposed to go with Aleksi. We talked about it so much and I will never see him there, just like you will never see Anna here again.

A small squirrel climbed onto their table and started to eat the immigrant's doughnut, as if wanting to tell them to cheer up and that happiness brings solutions.

Botum was shedding tears; the squirrel was eating the doughnut. The immigrant's head was swimming with thoughts whose meaning he could not grasp: - I almost get sad when I think of the things that she had promised me. She never said important things with words, only with looks. I wish I could embrace sorrow so that I can cry. I wish I could shed at least a tear. But the moment I get near the feeling of sorrow, it turns into movement. I am almost sad when I think of her. I just have to relax and everything will be alright.

Once I relax, I will feel sorrow and I will be happy because of it.-, the funny immigrant thought.

Restlessness

The train

While the train was passing through green solar
wind
I leaned against the window and closed my eyes
I dozed off and was startled when I noticed that a
man in his late thirties was sitting next to me
He did not look dreadful, or menacing, I was not
startled because of that
I simply did not expect anybody to be next to me
I leaned forward to look into his eyes and wish him
a good trip, when I realised I was looking at my
own reflection in the window
My appearance in the depth of the cold glass
The restless light behind my moving picture
The restless light the colour of a birch leaf was
going up, and then down to the ground
The souls of others

Please help me bring the wood. Take a basket. Thank you.

You see, people from all social classes and all parts of the world come here to the sauna. People of the entire planet! A few days ago a boy from Uruguay came; he told me that the word *tango* comes from Congo and it means a closed circle or space. Slave traders used the word for the places where they kept the slaves locked. The slaves also called their drums tangos. *Candombe* was their dance and music, and out of the music of black slaves the tango we know nowadays was born. You ask me about when tango came to Finland. We Finns, we've played tango for over a hundred years, and we dance it with our bodies close, in a slow, slow, fast, fast kind of step pattern.

The cosmic fires, the yellowing newspapers, Joni, Inka, You and me. The love of two friends who meet in the sauna. Panu's longing and Inka – her dance, so magnificent because of her commitment, because of the escape from oneself. The longing man, the longing music. Love inside a man, love inside a dance.

And our funny immigrants... Fearless!

We have a fantastic story full of losers.

Just like Panu was saying jokingly:

-My love life is a song, a fairy-tale, fictional, in one word: fantasy.

Speaking of love, some time ago a Greek boy came here. He told me that since ancient times Greek people have differentiated four types of love: relation or closeness, friendship, lust and divine.

Panu's love encompassed all those types.

25
An Important Guest

Aleksi was looking pensively out the window at the snow, ice and the blue sky. He seemed worried.

-Don't worry, Aleksi. Your belly makes you look good around your middle.-, Panu jovially said, which brought the answer:

-In the face of madness, I pretend to be normal.

Restless Panu was taken aback in all his immobility. Surprised, outwitted, he was waiting for the next sentence and got it:

-Nothing ever happens here!-, Aleksi said while he poured water over the hot stones.

-But maybe something will happen. I have a feeling.-, Panu answered.

Aleksi stood up and went to fetch the beer he had left outside. But, before returning to the hot sauna, he sat watching the frozen lake and the blue sky. The immobility was omnipresent and beautiful. He took a bit of snow and rubbed it against his body. He covered his face with snow and closed his eyes. When he opened them, the snow had already melted. And then the well-known feeling came, the feeling that always brought him back to sauna– the feeling of unity with the wind, with the winter, with the breath, the feeling where neither good nor bad exists, where nature does not know where reason starts. The feeling lasts until the frost slowly crawls back under the skin and into the bones, and it's time to return to the hot stones in the wooden box.

-Where have you been?–, Panu asked when Aleksi came back.

-I was outside, cooling the beer. Here you are, Lappish gold made out of Lappish water.

-The best beer in the world!

-The best in the world known to us, Panu.

Panu thought about how large the world was. He also thought about the stars beyond the blue dome. He removed his feet from the ceiling and sat up.

-You are not upside down anymore.–, Aleksi noticed.

Through the window, on the other side of the lake a greenish light appeared, meandering up and down. As a whole, it seemed as if it was made out of different beings. It seemed to dance and it seemed that it had some work to do. Northern lights are very rare during daylight. Panu sat next to Aleksi speechlessly watching nature in its magnificent theatre. On their faces, drunk with beauty, the colours of the sun were playing with the colours of the northern lights.

-Panu, do you ever plan to leave this village?

-Maybe, I don't know, though. I still have the fear of changing my environment. I fear that I would get lost and disappear. I know you can't understand that.

-I can understand that perfectly, Panu, absolutely. Even my ex-fiancée tricked me. I spent all my money to bring her here and she did not even show up.

-She is probably swimming on a beach on some southern sea now, thanks to your money.

-You're probably right. She's probably just an egoist.

-Okay, Aleksi, but maybe I am wrong! Maybe she is not swimming, maybe something completely different happened.

Panu and Aleksi were sitting next to each

other when they heard somebody knock. They both knew that an important guest was behind the door, as a lot of signs were predicting it.

Panu said with a serious and polite voice:

-Please come inside!-, and then he saw the important guest, in fact, so important that even Aleksi's heart was unprepared and wanted to jump out of the seemingly calm body.

26

The Tango Evening

Tampere

Botum had never been in a sauna before,
which is not a surprise, since the average
temperature in Cambodia is 27 degrees Celsius.

Botum had thought that sauna was a place
for cultural masochism, but she became interested
in visiting one when the immigrant explained that
sauna was instead a place of cultural hedonism.
They bought her a green swimsuit, resolute to try
winter swimming. He took her to the public sauna
that was simply called Rauhaniemen kansankylpylä,
located on a tiny peninsula on Näsijärvi lake. They
walked along a narrow path through the wood,
meeting passers-by who were looking at him and
his baggy, red-haired friend.

She, freshly showered, with a red wig and
him with a red beanie, sat on a wooden bench in
the hot steam looking at the white bodies that were
going in and out.

-I can't breathe.–, Botum said.

-It just seems so. The air is very hot, you'll
get used to it.

-I am burning, my ears are burning.-, Botum
was saying.

-Put the wig over your ears.

After the first sauna bath they went to the
ice hole in the lake. The funny immigrant swam a
few strokes. Botum did not want to swim. They sat

on a bench with beers, leaning against the wooden building.

   -I feel like a bird! And yet I am just sitting here.-, Botum said.

   -That's the high that you get from sauna.

   -Now I understand.- Botum smiled

   -A bird that doesn't fly.

   -A bird that swims in icy cold water.-, said Botum, sitting in the idyllic winter euphoria, looking at a group of young men who were singing to a friend dressed as a penguin.

   -A bachelor party. The guy that is dressed up as a penguin is getting married, and today he is supposed to do silly tasks from a list that his buddies made. It's a Finnish tradition.-, he explained briefly.

   The temperature in the sauna was exactly three times the average temperature in Cambodia. The gigantic penguin was sitting next to them. Nobody poured water on the stones, thinking that it may harm him. He stayed inside for a short time and went out. He was young and skinny. He left the costume lifelessly sitting on the bench with the back to the sauna wall. He swam in the cold water and left.

   -Are you afraid that your kidnappers will find you?-, he asked and saw Joni arriving to the ticket office to pay the entrance fee and buy some beers.

   -Even with my feet on the ground, I feel like I am flying. I believe the kidnappers will stick around the police station, thinking that that's where I would go. I have better things to do, like sit here and drink this beer, for example.

   They entered the sauna. Joni sat next to them and brought a can for each of them. The immigrant quickly explained how Botum was kidnapped and ran away, but Joni wasn't listening, which wasn't very unusual. He closed his eyes, lifted his arms, imagining a rope and himself walking across it, above the rapids in the centre of town.

Botum was looking at the hats that people in the sauna were wearing; hats in the shape of Angry Birds, pigs, Viking helmets... The immigrant was the only person with a normal red beanie, and Joni was the only person without a hat. He seemed to be immune to the heat of the steam even when it reached the top of his ears. He was lost in his own thoughts, high above the rapids, on the rope, balanced and yet so close to the ever-cold waters.

Distant from this story and events in it, Joni came back from his thoughts and suggested they go to the bar "Klubi" to a tango evening. He mentioned that he knew a guy called Simon, who is the organiser of the event and could get them in for free. The Serbian immigrant accepted the offer, seemingly unwillingly.

-Okay, not a bad idea!

Botum was really happy that they were going to a dancing event and, girl-like, worried about not having anything to wear. Joni told her to wear the penguin costume.

-Fantastic. Soon I'll know what it feels like to be a soon-to-be-married bachelor! - the fearless Cambodian girl joked.

The costume made Botum happy. Not because of what it looked like, but because it made her think that she would become a walking mascot. She will be present, but hidden.

In the dance hall, dressed up as a penguin, Botum danced so beautifully, that all the women who danced with her looked gorgeous. Dressed in a costume that suggested that she was male, she glided gracefully on the dance floor. Joni was looking at this gigantic bird and told her that she was beautiful. Joni spent short moments next to the immigrant, as he was in high demand to dance with the ladies in evening gowns; he danced with only a few short breaks. The Serbian immigrant was seated until the end of the evening, surrounded by the music of love and sorrow, covered with disco ball dots. He sat and looked around. The walls were covered with posters - they carried the face of Inka, and also the makeup advertisements that showed her smile. She was visible everywhere, while the immigrant was completely invisible in the music of sorrow and passion.

They stayed until the end of the evening and said goodbye to Joni who was talking to Simon, the organiser of the event, about Inka; Simon believed that Inka was in Argentina, teaching the Argentinians how to dance. The immigrant didn't find it unusual that Joni didn't know where Inka was, even though they were a couple until recently, but he did find it unusual that Joni would be interested in anybody else at all.

Botum and her host left. He walked with her, as if he was walking with a guy who fell out with his friends on the day of his bachelor party. A host and a groom; the lonely pathos of immigration.

-Do you know anybody from Cambodia who lives here in Finland?-, she asked, without taking the penguin head off.

-No. You are the only Cambodian that I know.-, he replied.

-Do you know anybody from Serbia?-, she asked as they walked along amongst the colours of busses, snow and drunks.

-I know Dušan.

-What does Dušan do here in Finland?

-He says that he's an engineer and that he

works for a company called Metso, but I don't believe him.

-You don't believe him?

-No, I even think he wears fake glasses to appear more intellectual.

-So what does he do, then?

-He does lonely, beautiful women.

-And how does that go?-, Botum was smiling, interested.

-There's an economic crisis, but his line of business is flourishing.

-Beautiful women, but lonely. What am I doing here?

-You are looking for love!-, he answered with genuine pathos.

-I should introduce Dušan to my mother; she is beautiful and has been very lonely since my father left us.

-What happened to him?-, he asked.

-A tiger attacked us.

-The tiger killed him?

-No, it didn't. I'll tell you later what happened.

Large snowflakes were falling on Hämeenkatu, the main street, the busses cruised the sea of snow, and the drunkards were hugging the imaginary warmth of love on the cold sidewalks.

27
Consumers

The train

The train sped through the dusk of a birch forest
Towards the road lit with frozen lampions
Next to the supermarket with large glass doors
The car park next to the heated cube held the weight of countless cars
And three colourful advertisements
The train slowed down, crawling along five million products, five thousand consumers, five serious, tired cashiers, who were reading the prices with the help of technology
As if the train wanted to admire the impersonal patchwork of objects that lured the consumers into making personal choices over things they do not really need
Creating an emptiness that must never be filled
Next to one of the lampions at the beginning of the forest, the elks were milling about
They were throwing hot steam out of their lungs into the icy air

Cosmic fires create all kinds of stuff, both good and bad, and they bring us big surprises. You are probably asking yourself which important guest they brought us. I will show you the newspapers. They have turned a bit yellow, but it doesn't matter. Come to my booth, where I sell tickets. Please come in.

Here they are, on that pile.

Not that pile. Those are newspapers with Joni in them. The tabloids were following him, mostly because of his relationship with Inka and his tightrope walking. People who want so much to be noticed are noticed, eventually. Some were saying that he was a cheat, some that he wasn't, but Joni didn't care. He cared about himself, his own existence and mortality. And the proofs that he existed and that he was finite were important to him. Always up there, but prone to falling. I know you know many people like that. True, Joni is one of them, and he appeared in the newspapers, which are yellow now with age.

And who can the important guest be, you are asking yourselves, although you know the answer. The papers are on the other side. Yes, it was Inka! I saw her yesterday. She is still beautiful, and she has lovely children. She is still the most beautiful. Yes, she is the important guest. Panu's flame came to the sauna in all her beauty, which was completely imperfect, insecure, fragile and unique, unsurpassed, absolute.

And now you are asking yourselves, and you don't know the answer, if Panu would ever be with her. You see, Panu didn't know it, but he was overjoyed just to be next to her. You see, our Finns are not as dumb as our immigrants who walk amidst the evil beasts dressed as penguins. Panu was not unrealistic, even though he was madly in love. Those loves worth dying for are the loves worth living for.

Inka

Sauna

Love comes and goes, like the leaves, like the snow, like a train, like laughter and tears. Love comes and goes in the body, in the memory, the same or changed. Love comes and goes. Inka arrived. She was standing in a red swimsuit. She was wearing green sunglasses; after the steam cleared it became obvious that they were actually blue. She was wearing a wide, joyful smile, or maybe it wasn't joyful, but it was gorgeous nevertheless.

-Hello guys!

-Inka! Inka!-, Panu happily went to give her a hug with his sauna-cooked body. Aleksi's face was serious, with large tears running down.

-Slow down Panu. Although I am coming with a large belly, I have lost lot of weight; I have become one third of myself. I can hardly stand.

-It's time to celebrate today!-, Panu shouted in the small wooden space. -And you don't need to be standing to celebrate!

-It's good to see good people!-, Inka said with the voice of a skinny angel. Aleksi didn't wipe his tears.

The materialised yearning. Happiness and sorrow were together in the Finnish sauna. Sorrow and happiness were giving warmth to the cold day, making the reality between the snow and the stars seem hazy. Contacts among friends show this best; Aleksi stood up and approached Inka, heavy-footed, reaching out his hand to her, as if he was agreeing on a bank loan.

-It's nice to see you Aleksi.-, Inka told him as they shook hands.

Aleksi remembered an old conversation and added:

-You are right Panu. Leaving is pointless if you have the right people next to you.

-A lot of things are pointless when you have the right people next to you. Education is pointless. Ambition is pointless.-, Panu agreed with himself.

-But beer isn't pointless at all! And we are not pointless.-, Aleksi added.

-Tell me Inka, promise me.-, Panu said gladly but seriously.

-Promise you what, Panu?

-Promise me that you will never leave.

Inka took off her glasses and her smile. She had black circles under her eyes, and they were not from makeup. The black looked like sleepless nights and days.

-I am staying forever.

Panu stormed out of the sauna into the minus many degrees Celsius. He came back carrying an accordion and an acoustic bass guitar. He was so fast that his friends didn't manage to drink even half of their beers.

-Musicians are coming soon.-, he said, turning the bucket upside down, thus converting it into a percussion instrument.

Three friends were drinking beer in the sauna, one of them frightened that he may be dreaming. The stones on the sauna stove were hot with joy, the wood was warm with love. Nobody slept in the sauna, next to the hot stove. Ambition was reduced to friendship, contact was reduced to friendship. The light became a cheerful observer.

The cosmic fires can look at the mascots without knowing who they are, and with incorrect conclusions. That's the way people were looking at the fearless penguin, thinking that it was a groom. Attracting attention to the fake self, Botum was hiding her real self. Fearless, petite, smart woman! She showed us all at least this little piece of wisdom: If you're not a tiger, at least be a penguin.

You find it funny, but I don't.

You see, I am neither a tiger, nor a penguin. But let's not talk about that now. I'm already too old to change.

As you heard, Panu was celebrating the object of his yearning that had just materialised in front of him. Palpable but untouchable, an unusual object of yearning.

31
Without and With

Without a job, without security, but with time. Full of passion. The doughnuts are tasteless. The funny immigrant went to buy food for himself and his guest. He told Botum he was taking a holiday.

He was walking along the street, on a cool cloudless day. The light was glaring, and his eyes were protected behind black sunglasses. He went to a bar on Otavalankatu and drank coffee from a glass. His winter sunglasses were on the table. In the reflection on the sunglasses he watched the coffee slowly disappear. People who entered were dressed too warm for the heat of the bar were coming and going.

When he returned with bread and milk in a thick paper bag, Botum asked him what his story was. He explained that he graduated from biology high school and that he is working on important experiments. He didn't want to say that he lost his job. He explained that he had been in a relationship with Anna for months, and that she was trying to talk him into having children but that he wasn't ready. For a few weeks she kept saying that she would leave and go back to Lapland. The last week they didn't talk at all, or see each other.

-So, she left!-, Botum said.

-She left.

-At least you know where to find her.

-I do.

-And what's your story, Botum?

-I come from Cambodia, from a small village

next to the sea. I love Finnish tango. I studied dancing in the school of a neighbouring city, and I like water skiing too. My favourite singer is Olavi Virta and my favourite dancer is Inka. Men in my village are skinny and scarce. I found Aleksi on the net, through some people who connected us via our interest in tango. They organised our dates on the net, and I gave a lot of money for the ticket and found myself in a place for prostitution, from which I ran away to you. I am in love with nature, love, sadness, countryside.

That's my story, in a nutshell.

-Why are you in love with sadness?- he asked, surprised.

-Sadness is wonderful, and it's even more wonderful to share sadness with a friend. -, she replied.

-Just like when you are dancing, just like tango?

-Just like tango.

Our funny immigrant reflected - how many days without seeing her? Ten. Ten is a number without much sense. Ten days away from her. Ten days she doesn't caress me with her eyes. Rented walls are just walls without her; they don't make a home. Entirety is empty and the furniture is without substance. The things are just objects without ideas when she is not around. Nature is a glance into its own insignificance. Biology is like physics of happening without the pursuit of the essence.-

-You sure got lost in reminiscence. I can see you miss her a lot.

-You are right.

-Do you miss Aleksi?

-I miss one very important thing about him.

-And what is that?

-I miss the thought that he is the right one for me.

-Maybe he is. Maybe he was tricked by the same people who scammed you.

-He didn't wait for me.

-Maybe Aleksi didn't know where and when to wait for you.

He saw a smile and a tear of joy. He looked through the window towards the lake: a boy and a girl were skating across the frozen surface. They had skiing poles and pushed themselves briskly. They had no destination. Aimless speeding with the person you love. They breathed the air deeply. They smiled with ruddy cheeks. They looked at each other through ski goggles. They skated and turned, so fast as if they were going downhill. Ice sparks followed them, like little stars in pursuit of the famous. The sparks were melting in the warmth of their love.

32
Nobody

The train

The train is passing by
I am nobody and I come from water and sun
I am nothing
I am nobody and I am enjoying it
When it's July, when it's December, I am nobody
I am nobody and I am nowhere
I am nothing that loves
The burning ice

The cosmic fires create things that we try to understand. They know about us, even though we are tiny. It might sound ego-centric, or earth-centric, but the little that we know shows us that life is so rare in the vastness of the universe and so precious; and preciousness can be random, but never negligible.

How about a shot of vodka? Don't conclude that I think that our planet is the only one that harbours life. No, I think there are many like ours, but what makes us precious is that our planet is the only one with life in the universe that we are aware of.

The cosmic fires enjoy friendly quarrels, the same as this quarrel between Panu and Aleksi. Those who quarrel love each other. And they quarrelled in the space where they spent the most time together - in the sauna. A friendly quarrel connects the hedonistic, decadent with the beautiful and wise.

Just like as Panu used to joke:

-I keep a close eye on good friends and on enemies; without them life would have no meaning.

I know, Panu says a lot of things, but sometimes he has a point. That's a skill too.

Let's continue about friends and sauna, about their love and the recently materialised object of yearning.

Justification, Friction, Fraction

Sauna

Panu was expectedly excited.

-I could dream about the wilderness, about animals in remote Africa, about beautiful Ethiopian women. I could daydream about faraway seas, corals and colourful fish. I could say that this world is wonderful, or that it is rotating in the opposite direction, but I am happy with you by my side, my friends. You are a very important reason for my existence here in this sauna. You, Aleksi and Inka.

Inka enjoyed hearing the kind words of a friend, but she was not hiding her surprise:

-I just came here, and you haven't left the sauna in years.

-You are more and more absurd, Panu.-, Aleksi added.

-I am very reasonable. I stayed here hoping that one day all my friends would come back.

-You can wait another hundred years, but it's hardly possible that all of us will gather again.-, Aleksi replied.

-Pay attention: Inka, you and me, that leaves only Anna and Joni. We have three fifths, that's 60 %. That makes me 60% right.

-You are wonderful Panu. You are a wonderful friend. It doesn't matter who is right and how much.

-The percentages don't matter, Panu. You are a wonderful friend.-, Aleksi agreed.

Panu felt the type of excitement that some people might call catharsis, the ultimate experience, just like when your heart is hit by a song or a particular note Confused, he went outside, to the minus degrees, to the wind, to calm down. He rubbed snow against his body. His gaze was lost in the nowhere, in the emptiness of the wild.

A few silhouettes were arriving from the wild, then the silhouettes became gangling creatures, the gangling creatures turned into human shapes, the human shapes became the musicians.

-Welcome! Inside we have a bucket that can serve as a drum, an accordion and an acoustic bass.

-We are carrying two guitars and a harmonica. Have any beer?-, one of the musicians asked.

-Of course! Lapin Kulta - the Lappish gold - the best one.

-We have vodka, but wouldn't like to use it, it's too early.

The musicians took their clothes off, showered, and put on their instruments. Sauna, with so many people inside, seemed even bigger than moments ago. The cold sky outside, seen from the inside, looked clean and joyful. Aleksi wore tears of joy on his face, again.

-Open the door a bit, to reduce the heat, because of the instruments.-, the quiet musician said.

Aleksi thought how the quiet musician looked like fake Elvis, just with a different haircut.

Panu stood up, went next to the stove and with a bottle in his hands, addressed the people present formally:

-The reason why I called the musicians is to celebrate this occasion.

Then he addressed Inka, who, as a celebrity

was used to formal situations, but not to this type of formality:

-Inka, you are a holy woman.-, Panu added: -I tell you, you will be celebrated in 50 and in 500 years. They will refer to you as a goddess, the goddess of Finnish tango.

-Panu, you are exaggerating, my friend!

The musicians started playing songs about happiness and sorrow, about love, god and death. Panu was playing percussion, hitting the bucket and surprising everybody with his skill. Inka was wearing a smile, and holding her belly with her hand; it didn't bother her that she returned in search of peace but found a noisy sauna full of love.

The musicians stopped playing for a moment and Panu stood up, again very formal:

-Cheers! Real people!-, he looked at the musicians and the beer and said: -My Lappish gold.

Aleksi wasn't drinking and wasn't happy like the others. Panu noticed it, saying:

-What now, you conceited person? You think you are better than others because you studied at university?

-No I don't, Panu.

-Yes you do, yes you do.

-No I don't.

-Now, since you are so smart, tell me one thing.

-What thing?-, Aleksi's face seemed sad.

-What is a fraction?

-It's division.

-You are clueless. So much studying for nothing. *Fraction*, coming from the Latin word fractus means broken, fractured, and represents a part of a whole or, more generally, any number of equal parts.

-Bravo! Everybody shouted, including Aleksi,

who finally lightened up. Maybe because of his merry face, that "bravo" was followed by a loud applause. It became obvious that the audience was performing in order to congratulate itself.

When the applause faded and the last resonance in the sauna dissipated, Inka said, with her slight smile bathed with friendship and goodness:

-I have a secret, and it's time to share it with you.

The musicians left their instruments and sat on the lowest bench, Panu and Aleksi sat next to them. They looked at Inka from below, as if they were looking at a deity that was about to reveal the secret of life.

Life comes, and life goes. Joni will soon die. Or disappear. After all this time I think he died. Life is all around us.

Would you like another shot? Koskenkorva! No?! It doesn't matter. I drink occasionally and I drink little. Only vodka, never beer. I got sick of beer when I went to Serbia once.

And our funny immigrants, in love with people who know each other, don't understand anything. They don't realise that Aleksi and Anna are from the same village, and they don't understand that Inka connects them, but it's just a matter of time when that will happen and they will head towards the village in Lapland. Love is in the sauna.

Fearless like a penguin, dressed to attract attention to her fake self, Botum could not decide what to do with herself; and the funny immigrant was waiting for Joni's performance, after which he wanted to head north. Joni forced him to promise that he would come to watch him.

People who are prone to falling need witnesses to justify their affinity.

Fearless like a penguin, Botum was dressed in a penguin costume. She would not be wearing it if she had known that Surma had caught up with her kidnappers, but, regardless of the reason, it was nice to see a giant bird walking around the town. A lost groom.

Let's see what our funny immigrants are doing.

Skiing

It was early morning, and the Serbian immigrant woke up at the usual time to go to work, even though he was on a so-called holiday. Botum was not asleep; she asked what the plan for the day was. Her funny host remembered that she had told him she loved water skiing. Good stuff for holiday, even this fake one. The price on Tuesdays for a ski lift in Sappee was 2 euros per hour, which is excellent for his tight budget and the amusement of his guest, although the physical state of the water she would ski on will be a bit different from what she was used to in Cambodia.

Botum was wearing the penguin costume. They arrived in the morning, which meant that it was still dark. The wooden cabins had lit lamps here and there. The narrow pathways between the cabins were decorated with short thick candles. Through the semi-darkness they saw the reflectors pour their light onto the ski slopes. Snow cannons were throwing snow, even though there was already more than enough of it everywhere. From the top of the slope, above the river of reflector lights, in the semi-darkness lay the frozen forest. It looked warm, even though it was frozen. Mild cold wind was hitting their faces. The snow was powder.

There weren't many people at Sappee, just a few teenagers who skipped school. The penguin friend was an excellent skier, or she seemed experienced, which led to the conclusion that water skiing was similar to downhill skiing, with a speedboat replaced by gravity. They spent several hours on the slopes, then they went to have lunch, and with the lunch they checked the tabloid news on its already-yellowing pages.

JONI – A CROOK?

WHERE IS INKA?

SKILL OR DECEPTION?

INKA LEFT JONI BECAUSE SHE DISCOVERED SOMETHING!

Inside the newspapers there were many theories, among them the one that claimed that Joni is attached with an invisible string while he is walking on the rope. Most of the articles were directed towards Joni's upcoming performance above the rapids between the two lakes in Tampere.

While the funny immigrant was leafing through the paper, Botum was impressed with the colossal fireplace in the centre of the restaurant where they were eating. She saw it as a grand, beautiful construction with a purpose of its own, to keep the rest of the building warm. Penguin often noticed the magic in the everyday, the magic that we don't even notice.

To add to the pleasure of their skiing experience, the penguin and its funny host went to a sauna.

Hot, holding a beer, the girl with a long red wig and the immigrant went out. He looked at the switched off lighthouse on the lake that was waiting for a warmer season, boats and ships.

The wind chased across the frozen water carrying white powder up to the pale blue sky. The land was winding impressively through the grey green lines visible under the whiteness of snow. The sky was clear, soaking the cold colours of the warm sun. Nearby the trees were standing, wrapped in snow, motionless, close to the people who were jumping into the hole made in the ice and running out, their hearts racing and their cheeks red.

He was one of them. His skin was icy but his body was hot.

He sat on a wooden bench, and Botum sat next to him. She did not want to swim in the frozen lake. People were sitting in front of them and drinking their beers. Nobody talked to him, nobody even looked at him. Suddenly he felt a thrill, the high that sauna gives after you go out into the cold. Then he felt the connection with the whole of nature, with people, with snow and sky.

Blonde Girls

The train

Youth and sport together, the beauty of smiles
The blonde girls took off their hats and jackets
They are sitting in their thin fleece ski tops
They say that the beginning was a long time ago
Small and insignificant, almost invisible
But important in the burst of its unrest
Maybe the unrest of the beginning is inside me
When the cosmic fires started their wandering
And turned into life, into tracks and trains
Into choo-chooing and uniforms
Into beautiful blonde girls
Oh, so beautiful blonde girls

Are you sure you don't want another shot? Koskenkorva! Yes! Great. I drink little and occasionally. Only vodka, never beer. Come with me, I will set the fire in the stove. It won't take long. It got really cold today, just like yesterday, the minus does not change that easily here. It doesn't change and I don't want it to change either.

I remember Panu saying jokingly:

-I needed a change, so I went to the sauna, and stayed there.

Sometimes he also used to say:

-My life had no content; this is why I was going to sauna every day, where I was looking at my friend who was saying that nothing was ever happening.

Panu was not right, because his life was full of love. It's clear to me now. We start appreciating things only after we lose them.

You are probably interested what people without love are like, what the kidnappers are like. You see, I spend a lot of time in this little house. I have thought about them a lot.

The Kidnappers and the Fifth Girl

The boss was sitting with his workers, explaining to them how, very soon, maybe even next year they would reach financial stability.

-We now have four girls, and the fifth one is coming. Bit by bit...

-Boss. I just checked the car, I'm a bit worried.

-Don't worry. Next year we'll have a better car. All our profit goes to our costs now. The initial investment in our business will bring returns soon. And after, you will be working 7,5 hours a day, with paid holiday and days off, all according to the law. We won't be driving this piece of rubbish. -, the boss wisely replied, and then asked

-Is the heating working in the car now?

-It's working, boss.

-It's working. Harmony, you see. Everything is okay. Massage and faith, that's the connection. The massage is ancient and it relaxes the muscles, increases efficiency of connective tissues and energy flow inside the body. Faith gives meaning to our existence. Massage and faith! That's the deal!

-And how is our god called?-, asked the other kidnapper.

-The name has no importance. There is only one god; people just give him different names. What matters is that god helps us. God creates the order and we help him in it.

-And the girls are our servants?

-They don't have it that bad. Imagine how

many hungry people there are in the world. The girls, on the contrary, have great bodies and are not hungry.

-I'm not worried about them, boss, I'm worried about us. I don't think the car will make it to Helsinki.

-We'll buy a four-wheel drive. Next year. Just take it easy. God sees everything, I'm sure success is waiting for us.

It's unbelievable how bad people connect themselves to a higher power to give their own evil justifications of faith and harmony. Nothing new, I know. The kidnappers in this case, however, have created a combination of massage and faith, a silly connection, you have to admit.

How did the evil become evil? I think something twisted their feeling of compassion; probably it was a lack of love and warped perception of values.

Let's talk about love! Let's go back to the friends and musicians in the sauna. Let's go back to Panu's materialised object of yearning who will tell them a beautiful secret.

The sauna was hot, and the door was a bit ajar, so that the musicians could play. Let's peek inside.

Evolution

Sauna

-I'm pregnant, as you could probably notice.-, Inka held her hand over her small belly.

-I could not notice!-, Panu did not even congratulate.

-Congratulations, Inka!-, Aleksi remembered.

-Congratulations!-, the musicians and Panu said, looking at Inka as if she were a goddess of dance and fertility.

-I want to make it clear to everybody here that I am not the father, but I can become one if it's needed!-, Panu wanted to make up for the previous delay in reacting.

-Thank you Panu. The father of the child is far away now, and I am not sure if the child will ever see him.

Panu left the men on the bottom bench and stood up. He approached the stove and started pouring water over the stones, slowly and onto one spot, without saying anything:

-I never wanted to complain, at least not publicly, and that's the reason why I am saying this to you Aleksi, now, with these people as witnesses.

-Say it, Panu.

-You have really tired me with your whining. Come on, relax a bit. Let's have a drink. The gentlemen here will play some music for us. Do you know how many years of practicing and evolution it takes to play an instrument?

-I don't know, Panu. Come on, enlighten me.-, Aleksi was enjoying the digressive monologue of his friend. He listened to him with a smile of approval on his face.

-You keep saying how nothing is ever happening around here, while we are looking at the ice and snow through the window, and we are creating a microclimate inside here. We are changing the physical state of water. The magic of nature. Look!-, and the recently-dispirited Panu became ecstatic.

-Are the physical states events?-, Aleksi asked, just for the sake of saying something, but Panu didn't reply.

Inka was looking at her old friends.

-I can see that nothing has changed around here.

-Everything has changed. You are pregnant, for which I congratulate you again. We have *evolved*.

We've evolved into adults. Into witnesses of planetary events, and of the changes of physical states of matter.

The blue planet was circling routinely, apparently not changing its path. From the restlessness of the Big Bang stardust and thoughts came. The planet moved in its turmoil of creation through the universe that was larger than all thoughts ever thought.

In the heat of the sauna, one friend, Aleksi, asked Inka:

-Who is the father of the child?

Who was the tiger? You don't know.

Was it really an animal from the wilderness, or just anger that is created when sadness is repressed? What attacked Botum's father, and what makes us hide our own sorrow from ourselves? Maybe it's shame. Imposed shame! So we build temples and churches to impress ourselves and to have a place where we can be afraid and where we can be sad. Well, you see, when you dance tango, it's perfectly fine to be sad; you are sharing the sadness with your dance partner.

The cosmic fires can look at our sorrow and shame. I want to believe that they know, I want to believe that they feel.

Does that tiger, the one which attacks others, also attack us, ourselves? Yes, I'm thinking about Joni. Was he attacked by his own inner tiger? You are reading my mind. He probably was.

And what do the cosmic fires do? And what do they create? You don't know it. I wish they knew.

I don't know. I'm neither a penguin nor a tiger!

I am the yearning!

How about a shot of vodka? Yes?! You're wonderful.

Let's see what our immigrants are doing.

43
The Tiger

Tampere

They woke up to a new day. It was morning, which means they were stretching out in darkness. He asked her about the tiger and her father:

-Will you tell me about the tiger and your father?-, but Botum didn't answer.

-Let's visit Tampere Cathedral, and then go to sauna.-, she changed the topic.

-Alright.

-I like the stone that the temple is made of. I want to see what it's like inside.

-Let's go!

She put on her penguin costume and put on the red wig. They visited Tampere Cathedral, Tuomiokirkko, and looked at the stones shaped by the thoughts of Lars Sonck. They looked at Hugo Simberg's paintings; the fallen angel looked so ill that the funny immigrant wanted to enter the painting and help him, but luckily he was carried in children's arms. The next painting showed skeletons carefully watering a garden. This image of a small, caring Death brought Botum to tears, when the immigrant told her that they should celebrate life, because the awareness of existence is magnificent. Then she sat and looked at the painting behind the altar.

Too many impressions for the petite Buddhist, dressed in a Finnish bachelor party costume.

They went out. The snow covered the

church; you could see it in the morning darkness. It was falling when the bells started tolling. The fear and salvation stayed behind them. They walked on un-trampled snow. Lost birds were following their steps.

Only then did she reply to his question about the tiger and her father.

She said that she was playing in the village, next to her father, near the thick, humid jungle. The branches and green leaves were behind her when a large tiger appeared. It was an adult animal weighing 250 kilograms. Her father didn't take her in his arms and start running; instead he turned towards the tiger. The father wasn't shouting, he just said that the tiger made a mistake and that he would take its eyes out. Tiger is a hunter and it knows that it can take down a man, and it started running fast to attack. The father slowly walked towards the tiger, and while his left hand was inside tiger's jaws, while the fangs were breaking its skin and bones, the fingers of his right hand were in tiger's eyes. Then the rest of the villagers appeared and killed the tiger using a rifle, clubs and spears. Then they hung him from a tree in the jungle near the village, so that other dangerous animals would know that humans are the most dangerous animals.

-When my father recovered, he left our family because he was haunted by something.

The penguin and the immigrant walked for a long time. Penguins have no fear.

Penguins are faithful friends and spouses. They live far away in the southern hemisphere, not because they enjoy the coldness, but because there they have few enemies and many friends.

Penguins are not afraid; that is why they are never in the places where there is evil.

Penguins live in the tropics too, on the Galapagos Islands, which are on the Equator, and they are having a great time there.

And when a tiger attacks a penguin, it doesn't know that it is in for trouble.

They were near the rapids, near the bridge, where Joni was about to perform. They were walking when Botum said that she would wait for him in the apartment, because she saw the beautiful sorrow on his face and realised that he needed to be on his own.

The penguin went home, and the immigrant continued through the city lights that played with large snowflakes, and even the blue, the light of darkest desires, looked pretty through the snowflakes. He was walking between the two lakes. He breathed in the fresh air, crossing the Hämeensilta bridge. He was walking on the white, pristine street, among the inebriated souls. The snow fell in front of his steps. He looked at the jolly statues made by Wäinö Aaltonen long before he was able to even walk. The Finnish Maiden, The Tax Collector, The Hunter and The Merchant were looking at him. I am probably a lost soul too, a lost bird, only without beer inside of me, he thought.

He walked along the streets that they used to walk along together. He was just a body. He passed by the place that Anna used to go to, but he didn't, where the fragrances are mixed in small bottles. He met a girl that looked like her. She gave him a look and a smile. She looked him in the eyes while she was passing by. She even touched him, accidentally. That touch wasn't her touch, Anna's. As if the soul of the funny immigrant had left his body, and the body went to search for it, not knowing where.

Steam

The train

To grow and to grow up
To become strong
To grow old
To grow old with the love of the ones you love
To grow weak
To become dust
To become atom and subatomic particle
To become the train
To become water that disappears on the hot stones
of a sauna
To become light
Green light of the northern wind

I'm a bit bothered by the fact that I'm not totally sure that Joni is the father of Inka's child. After all these years, I am looking at the little girl's face and I am asking myself if I am trying to convince myself that it's Joni I see. He was Panu's friend but then he left him and then he left all of us. He never called him when he went to Tampere; he had better things to do. Panu heard about him from Aleksi.

Some people say: -Friends come and friends go.- I wasn't like that then, and I'm not like that now.

I am the yearning.

And next to their sauna is Life, on planks, on skis, as powerful as a strong dragon.

Next to Life there was Death, as it usually happens, the horrible death called Surma. But, before we go for a walk over the lake with the friends, let's see how the kidnappers got there.

The Kidnappers at the Airport

-Is she arriving soon?

-Soon.-, the boss replied.

-What's her name?

-Botum, which means *princess* in Khmer language.

-Funny. Her highness from Cambodia is coming. And she doesn't suspect what's awaiting her.-, the kidnapper was happy.

-What if she runs away?-, the other kidnapper asked.

-As soon as she arrives we'll take her passport, then we'll threaten to kill her mother if she runs away. God is merciful, he knows our woes and he will help us, so that she won't run away.-, spoke the boss wisely.

-But what if, by some chance, she escapes? What *if* that happens?

-God's wrath will fall on her. Is she giving us a choice, if she escapes?-, the boss wisely asked.

-She isn't.

-Correct. We'll need to eliminate first her mother, then her. -, the boss replied.

-You are right, boss.

-Although I don't believe that she would dare misbehave by escaping.-, the other kidnapper said.

-I don't believe that either, but there are all kinds of women.-, said the boss with a dumb expression on his face.

A Walk on the Lake

Sauna

Inka didn't reply to the question about who the child's father was, even though one of the musicians was sitting in a yoga pose and was looking at her as if she was Parvati. The blue planet was turning as always, and Panu sat on the lowest bench again, awaiting Inka's reply. Inka smiled, and in the eyes of her friends and musicians she was as beautiful as all of the beauty of the universe itself.

-I can't tell you! It's complicated!-Of course it's simple! We learned about it in biology lessons! And when it comes to the question who the father is, I know I'm not but I can become one!-, Panu stood up again and started pouring water over the sauna stones.

-Thank you Panu, my adorable friend!-, Inka said with a smile.

-Any time!-, Panu winked ecstatically.

-It's getting really hot in here!-, Aleksi added, blowing into his own fingers.

The heat and the humidity started crawling up the walls, the ceiling and the corners. The heat and the humidity approached the backs and the ears. Panu climbed to the top bench, stood up and remained bent, with his head touching the wooden ceiling. Smiling, he looked at the others leave sauna, only to follow them shortly. Inka was wrapped in her towel, while the others were walking around in their swimsuits.

The heated sauna goers started walking over the lake, on the hardened water.

-Look!-, Aleksi pointed to the other side of the lake.

-Surfers.-, the musician answered.-They come from Tampere.

Nearby were people with kites, racing over the surface of the frozen lake on skis and boards. The heated sauna goers went further towards the middle of the lake to see the surfers better, but the surfers were sailing further away because the sauna goers were walking too slowly. Then they saw something unexpected.

A frozen car.

Panu took Inka's towel for a moment, wrapped it around his hand and opened the car door.

-Calm down Inka, I'm sure they can't do us any harm. -, Aleksi said in a low voice.

-Don't look.-, Panu hugged Inka.

-Let me take this guy's phone. I'll call the police now!-, the quiet musician said.

-It's time to go.-, the other musician said. They went back to the sauna to take their things. They were frightened.

Inside the car, there was something horrible, something that made Inka scream, and the others look in disbelief and want to leave the place fast. Above the car, the sky was blue, it carried no clouds; it allowed the sun rays to shine on the witnesses of creation, existence and disappearance.

I am neither a tiger nor a penguin. But I know what a village is and I know what love is. I also know that Botum is about to realise where Aleksi is.

How about a shot of vodka? Yes?! Wonderful! Have a seat here, next to the yellowed newspapers, next to the yellowed tabloids.

I also know that the funny immigrant will go with her. The pathos of immigration! The top of the rock-bottom! Stealing from us what we never had!

I was once in that Serbia of his! I got sick of beer there. I'll tell you about that later! We have time.

The immigrant will soon have a moment of honesty, and then he will understand.Oh, how difficult it is to be honest! How difficult it is to be sad.

49
The Decision

Tampere

And after the sauna, the good old feeling.

The feeling of cold water wrapping the body. The feet are walking, while the body starts feeling weightless. The movements are slow and

breathing is deep, while the eyes are wandering over the frozen landscape. The exit is light and gives you a feeling of tallness and pain in your feet. And when the pain disappears your whole being is as light as air.

Filled with pleasure, the funny immigrant reached for his beer. And as if giving proof that life is inside, the coldness slowly starts getting inside the body. Slowly. Every sip is ancient, as if in an old ritual.

He was leafing through a tabloid today. It said:

INKA PREGNANT AND RETURNING TO FAMILY LIFE

IS JONI A FAKE?

JONI TO PERFORM IN THE CENTER OF TAMPERE!

Botum in the long red wing said that she missed Aleksi:

-I miss Aleksi! Now I understand.

He asked her what she missed the most about him:

-What do you miss the most about him?

-I miss our conversations about our dreams. Aleksi doesn't know how to dance, and I want to teach him how to dance Finnish tango.

Then she said that Aleksi knew Inka. -Inka and Aleksi come from the same village in Lapland.

To which the funny immigrant replied that Anna also knew Inka.-Anna and Inka come from the same village in Lapland.-, he continued: - Both you and Aleksi have been scammed. Aleksi is probably sitting in a sauna now, with the same misapprehension that you had.

Botum looked at him smiling. Leaning against the wooden outside wall, he said:

-It's all clear now. Both of us are going to Lapland.

-What about your job?

-I don't have it anymore. And I've never been a biologist, I did manual work.

-Great. We're going together.

-We'll go by train after Joni's performance. I promised to watch him.

He stared into the distance.

-What's on your mind now? What would you tell Anna now, before leaving?-, the red haired Botum was curious in a very girly way.

-Even though I'm an immigrant, even though I'm useless and uneducated, even though I'm madly in love, I'd tell her It's great without her, except when it's snowing.

And I don't think about her at all, except when I hear any female voice. And that I forgot about her, only the snowflakes remind me.

I don't remember her beautiful smile, her hug, I have completely forgotten her.

If only it wasn't snowing.

I feel great without her, just as I'd thought I

would. Except that her name is following me, like an invisible aura.

The Touch

The Train

I want to feel the touch of a woman
Gentle touch
The tremors of the tracks are reminding me
The edge of the curtain on my face is reminding me
of my desire

The world is changing. I read yesterday that this world is made of 119 elements, nine more than we knew about until recently. In fact, the elements have always been in and around us, since the moment the cosmic fires started their journey. We are discovering the elements. The world is changing. Or maybe we are changing, relative to the world! We are discovering and understanding things.

Aleksi will soon understand that Botum is looking for him, and that she will find him soon. Actually, Panu will tell him that.

Panu will soon understand that as a man, he is a double zero. Actually, Aleksi will tell him that.

But before we peek into their sauna again, I have to tell you something that happened earlier, regarding the musicians:

52
Musicians at the Blue Station on the Blue Horizon
A Concert for Inka

The musicians were sitting inside the warm train station. Two of them were angry at themselves; the third one was peaceful and quiet. I don't even know why they were so angry; they were simply that way. The musicians were looking out of the window, towards the lake, across which a madman in shorts and jacket was running. The madman was Panu. The steam swirled away from his body, you could see that he had just come out of the sauna.

-People, let's celebrate.

-Why would we celebrate?-, the quiet musician calmly asked.

Before answering, Panu thought that the musician looked like Elvis, although he was blonde.

-My friend returned.-, Panu said.

-A celebration requires specific preparations. We don't even have all the instruments with us now.-, one of the angry musicians said.

-Inka returned!-, Panu's face changed into a smile.

-Inka. We're coming!-, the musicians said, almost at the same time, all the faces smiling.

-Thank you. I have some instruments. I'll bring them to the sauna.

Panu ran back. The steam was still rising his body. His feet seemed to fly across the frozen water. Yes, he was abnormal, but joyful and madly in love.

53
The Zero Zero Man

Sauna

It seemed to Inka that a large golden bird flew onto the sauna's window sill. A golden bird next to the half steamy window. It stayed like that for a few minutes, looking into the sauna. It jumped away, fluttered and flew away. Inka thought that the bird flew away from somebody's cage. She stood up and went out to catch the poor lost bird that was looking for freedom in the wrong place. The freedom of movement in inhospitable surroundings. The freedom of movement in surroundings that can't stand you. The colourful freedom that Inka was looking for, while she was walking barefoot on the snow. She looked for the bird, but it wasn't on the window, so she returned.

It was boiling inside the sauna again. Panu was pouring water over the solid lava, saying:

-They are finding mammoths in remote parts of Siberia.

-What do mammoths have to do with what we just saw?

-They have everything to do with it. The mammoths got frozen and the armed people got frozen. Frozen like statues!-, Panu answered and added: -In Siberia they have mammoths, in Lapland we have statues, you see.

-You've gone completely mad, Panu.-, Aleksi said.

-Maybe, but it's interesting how many signs we've seen.

-What signs?-, Inka asked.

-There were three of them; that's the first sign.

They seem to be from southeast Asia; that's the second sign.

They were armed; the third sign.

They got lost looking for somebody; the fourth sign.

The person they were looking for is probably somebody from southeast Asia too; fifth sign.

I could continue listing the signs, but I expect Aleksi to finally react.

-React?

-Yes, it looks like you went to university for nothing. Your brain is not really working.

-Botum?

-Yes, the woman from the net.

-I'm going to look for her now.

-Stop and think, Aleksi.

-She is coming here, the frozen monuments were looking for her.-, Panu told him to wait.

-I'd expect somebody would cry for them.

-They are human zeros!-, Panu said: -Slaveholders. Merchants of lives, of young lives. I cannot feel sorry for them.

-They used to be children, just like us, Panu. But something made them take the wrong path in life. I feel sorry Panu, that both they and we all made wrong turns.

We - alienated, they - tarnished.

Panu was confused. He breathed heavily and went out.

The vast frozen lake stood underneath the clearest sky of blue. Inka went for a cold shower, while Panu approached the door and opened it a bit. Drops of cold water were jumping off Inka's small body and her beautiful face with large eye bags.

Aleksi saw how Panu looked at her and said:

-You are a zero zero man. You should realise that she is free, and not yours, and the world is not yours; stop controlling your own restlessness. Move!

Inka heard them; she hugged Aleksi and Panu and wanted to cry. But the tears didn't come. She thought again how the people frozen in that car used to be children a long time ago. She wondered what would make children turn out that way. Not only on this geographical path to Lapland, but to a life of crime. And who is that, who is the woman from the net, she wondered silently. She was thinking about the reasons and then she remembered the reason she returned here.

If you are wondering when and how Botum realised she had been kidnapped, the answer is immediately after she arrived. Here's how it happened:

The Kidnappers and the Awakening

-Welcome to Finland! Are you here for the first time?-, the boss asked as they were walking towards the car.

-It's my first time in Europe. I thought Aleksi would wait for me.

-Aleksi is busy. Your passport, please.-, the boss said as they were driving to Tampere.

-Here you are. Why are you taking it?

-We are the middlemen; we need to have all the documentation.

-Where is Aleksi?

-He is waiting for you in Tampere. He couldn't make it to the airport.-, the boss was saying as they were driving on the frozen highway to Tampere.

-Please come in your room. You will share it with this girl. Tomorrow will be your first working day. Dinner is on the table, I know you are hungry. If you run away we are going to kill your mother first, and then you, after we find you. Eat now. And get some rest.-, the boss said in the room with the other girl.

The blue neon lights were coming through

the window, and the snowflakes flew through the blue light to hit the window of the room.

The cosmic fires are aggressive. Nature is aggressive in her creation and in her destruction. When sorrow is suppressed, anger is created; destructive suicidal aggression.

You see, I'm neither a tiger nor a penguin. I'm talking about Joni.

Joni will soon die.

Life comes, life goes.

Joni is going.

56
Above the Abyss

Tampere

Even much earlier, there was vicious gossip that Joni was a faker. It claimed that he always performed at night so that the wire that is connected to his back wouldn't be visible. Or that he is using some material that doesn't reflect light. They were saying all kinds of things. And all was published on the internet and in the tabloids. More often, there was a question mark next to the newspaper story titles that were about him. The Genius of Balance? A Tightrope Walker? Courage? Deceit? There were also story titles without the question marks, and they were usually very long, such as: "The newspapers used to write about serious and dedicated people, like Elvira Madigan, now they are interested in fakers like Joni."

Just like every day, snow and ice were everywhere you looked. But this day was a special day because the genius or faker was walking a tightrope over the rapids that connects the two lakes. Fast moving water does not freeze easily, and the dramatic effect of it pouring over the sculpted ice under the reflectors was a great backdrop for the evening's performance.

People were arriving, from babies in prams to old ladies in wheelchairs, and all those in between. Large snowflakes onto the warm clothes. Even though it was still daytime, the reflectors were chasing the crystal structures over the streetlamps.

Large snowflakes at a pleasant minus 8 Celsius. Nordic celebration. Excited children in overalls were holding their parents by the hand. They looked like tiny astronauts, and their parents looked like cosmic balloons. The music soon started, and the large loudspeakers were pouring the music of jolly violins as a background to somebody who might fall. The music would remain jolly, even if somebody would fall, because it is the possibility of it that attracts the spectators. The snow would still be playing in the wind. Large snowflakes above people in warm clothing. Above the local televsion crews, the ambulance and the police.

Joni came to greet the penguin and the funny immigrant who were part of the crowd. Soon they were struggling to see him as he slowly made his way along the rope over the rapids. They could hear comments from those nearby:

-Look at the way Joni walks.

-It looks like the wind is swinging him.

-Do you think he has an invisible safety line?

-Joni is walking very carefully.

-Rope is moving a lot, seems that the wind is very strong.

-It's warm today, only -8.

-Joni is going to fall, he's losing control.

-His pole fell into the rapids, what is he going to do now?

-He's spreading his arms.

-He's falling! He's falling!

Even the fall didn't seem real. Dressed in a black suit, wearing an old-fashioned hat, he looked like a tango dancer, not a tightrope walker. Joni was falling as if it was a magician's trick. Half bent while falling, he tried to catch the hat. Half-bent, he tried to adjust the picture of himself, while cold water waited for him below. The hat will not keep you warm; it won't help in the ice cold water.

-Look, he's in the water! He fell! Joni fell!

The penguin and the funny immigrant started walking through the crowd towards the lower bridge, watching the water, but they couldn't find him. They searched for the ambulance, but they couldn't find it. There was only snow, large snowflakes dancing in the wind and falling on the structures of town buildings lit by the streetlights. Looking at the city, they tried hard to see all, but they couldn't see anything. They could only see the beautiful structures that were staring, indifferent to good and evil.

My Destiny

The Train

My Destiny
Heat without a stove
With a smile on your face
Enrage me not
My Destiny
Steam of the sauna
Calm wilderness
I'm moving on a train
Enrage me not

Snow is the light of our world! It's like every single snowflake tries to be prettier than the previous one. The snow is telling us where to walk; it doesn't cover, it uncovers. Snow is the light of our world.

The cosmic fires are flying, creating and destroying without empathy. They don't know about good and evil. We do know, and we are a part of the universe, we're made of the same elements.

The sky is grey, vodka is clear and transparent. Would you like a shot? Yes?! You're wonderful!

The grown children met in the sauna of their childhood. The funny grown children hid in the sauna of their childhood.

Anna will soon arrive, she will materialise in that small wooden box. Only one child was missing, but statistically, the cosmic fires are doing a good job; the universe is expanding, new lives are created, Inka was bringing a new life - a lovely girl.

You see, I am neither a tiger, nor a penguin. I'm not a fighter; I don't bind people, nor am I a groom.

The world is changing, everything is changing, except me, I am the yearning. The world is changing and people are prone to forgetting.

59

Musicians at a Railway Station on the Blue Horizon
Oblivion

The musicians were sitting inside the warm railway station. Two of them were angry at themselves; the third one was quiet and calm.

-I don't even know how we got here, in the first place!-, one of the angry musicians said.

Nobody answered. The silence annoyed him, so the angry musician said again:

-And our band's name is so dumb - "Acoustic Sauna"! - Our name is not even a Finnish name.

-I devised it. Every time somebody searches "Acoustic Sauna" on the internet, they will find us.-, the other angry musician said.

-And what exactly are they going to find? We've recorded nothing.

-I don't even know how we got here, in the first place!-, the other angry musician said.

-This was your idea, after our first performance at the festival.

-Maybe, I don't remember.

One Child Is Missing

Sauna

Lethargic until recently, but now ecstatic, Panu continued:

-We came to the earth, the earth is our mother. We prayed to the stones, the stone is our god. We followed the reindeer; we lived and died next to them. They lived and died next to us. We followed them, they didn't follow us. Our souls were becoming green light. Our ancestors were coming back to give us beauty. Our dogs were faithful to us. And we were faithful to them. We were together. We lived together in the winter, waiting for the spring. Nobody stole our springs. We waited for it and it came, every year. We came to the earth and we never left it.-, Panu added more water to the heat.

-And what can we do about it? The world is changing, and we respect our past. Something else is bothering you, Panu!

-What's bothering me, Aleksi?

-You've waited for years for Inka to come back, but now that she is back you realise that she is never going to be yours. You don't own the past, and you don't own the people. They are free.

Panu, who was sitting on the highest sauna bench, looked towards Inka, towards her mild smile, and said to her, in all his exaggerated self:

- I could talk about beauty for years, maybe even endlessly and I would not come to a conclusion about what beauty is. But what I am most enchanted with, about you, is your smile; it looks like it collected all the joy of the universe to give it to those you smile at. Every time you smile, I am happy to be alive.

-Thank you Panu, but, believe me, the world is much larger than my smile!-, Inka replied.

And as a confirmation that the world much larger than our perception of it, the small wooden space was suddenly filled with:

-Surprise!

It was a female voice, the voice of a jolly angel would be how we'd imagine it, that came from Tampere, from the place where the best doughnuts in the world are made.

-Surprise!

-Anna, Aleksi, Inka and me! Only one child is missing! Only one child is missing!-, Panu was delighted. He stood up from his throne from which he was throwing water, and hugged Anna.

Aleksi was looking at her with a serious face, down which, one single unwiped tear was rolling. Inka was holding her tiny belly, which she was calling huge; it was obvious that she had known Anna was back in the village and that the two of them had already met.

-Surprise!-, Anna repeated.

-Anna, it's nice to see you! I'm really happy that you are among us!

-I'm happy to be among you!-, Anna replied.

With his tear-stained face, Aleksi brought beers for everyone and quietly said:

-Welcome home.

-Thank you, Aleksi.

The four friends were drinking beer in the sauna, one of them afraid that it was all just a dream. The sauna stones were hot with joy, the wood was hot with love. In the sauna, next to the hot stove nobody was sleeping. Ambition was reduced to friendship, touch was reduced to friendship. The light became a jolly witness of it all.

-Only one child is missing! Only one child is missing!-, Panu was shouting forgetting about the tiny belly that Inka thought was huge and about the child inside, the new life.

On the sauna door you could see marks of age, as if they were writings about history. It was obvious that the edges of the door were finished by somebody's hand, meticulously and with patience. The door separated two worlds. The world of beautiful whiteness surrounded the world of the wonderful people in the sauna. Heat and cold, next to each other. Friendship and aloofness. Complete indifference and complete dedication. The whole world separated by a wooden door.

61

The smell of the forest, I can see it in my eyes! Somebody told me that they can smell the sea even if they see it on a postcard. You see, it's the same with me and forest. Look! On the left - trees that are becoming a forest. Look up, to the other side - the forest is climbing a hill. The wind isn't strong today. Can you smell it? I know, it's more difficult to smell it in winter. It's stronger in summer, it's almost like we are swimming in it.

You see, a long time ago Panu was saying:

-The woman understands that she is stranded only after she sails into the harbour of marriage.

But Inka wasn't married and yet she was stranded.

Do the cosmic fires care about our story, even though it's part of them and it is developing as they are flying? I know what you're thinking - you think they don't care.

Where is our story at? Let's see.

Botum ran away from the "massage with a happy ending" place and met a Serbian immigrant. It took them a bit of time to realise they both needed to go to Lapland, and they are about to go.

Anna left her job making doughnuts and, disappointed by the immigrant's immaturity, returned home, which impacted the quality of the doughnuts a lot. I don't find it funny.

Will Aleksi ever be with Botum? Will Panu ever be with Inka? Not even Panu knew that.

The kidnappers were killed in the battle against love, Surma caught up with them.

Inka has brought new life inside her. Her friends organised a small concert in her honour.

Joni has died. The immigrants will look for him, but they won't find him. Friends appear and disappear, and you cannot find them.

62
The Search

Tampere

-Let's go look for him!
-Look for him where?
-At the emergency room? In hospitals? At the police station?
-I can't go to the police.
-We'll call them. Let's first go to the emergency room.
-Ok. Let's go by bus, I don't have money for a taxi, because I need all the money I have left to buy us tickets to Lapland.
-Let's go!

The immigrants went to the emergency room of the town that night, but they didn't find Joni.

They searched for him, but they didn't want to find him. As if finding him would mean that they would find that he died. The funny immigrant wanted to believe that a group of drunken friends found him and took him to a sauna to get warm. Some special sauna, like the smoke sauna near Ylöjärvi. He wanted to believe that Joni was drinking beer now, and that he decided never to walk the rope again.

It felt strange that life outside continued as if nothing had happened. As if the metal halogen reflectors and the LED lights were witnesses of movement. As if the wheels are turning without any sense. As if the world didn't care what the outcome of the search would be. Sauna was a comfort; sauna and beer. And the thought of drunken company. They searched in the public hospitals, which directed them to check the private ones too, who, in turn, directed them to check at the police station. When the immigrant called the police they told him that they have no information about Joni. It looked like everything was okay and Joni hadn't fallen into the cold water. As if he was neither lost, nor saved. Like a magic trick, but without the evidence that it was just a trick.

They were returning from the hospital towards the centre of town, on a bus. The penguin and the funny immigrant were not saying a word. Botum had a sad smile, so beautiful.

It was dark and hot on the bus when the noise was heard - new passengers were getting on board. They were jolly and loud; a group of boys were singing to a group of girls. It seemed that the girls didn't know them and that they were pleasantly shy. Some lives fade away, and some were about to meet to create new lives. The planet is moving, the bus is moving, life is moving. The impossible disappearance, the change of state. Dead, alive. Seemingly motionless.

Botum was shedding tears over her smile. Never intrusive, not even now.

-Do you miss Anna?-, Botum asked quietly.

He wanted to reply to her -I was ready to give up everything for her love. Anna showed me how to swim in cold water. She would go down the few steps into the hole in the ice at the Rauhaniemi rock, swim a few strokes and slowly walk up the stairs out of the water and back to get warm in the sauna. I would go behind her, seemingly strong, with my chest up. But in fact I felt like a frozen mouse. Inside the sauna, at a wonderful 100 degrees Celsius, I asked her what else she wanted from me. What more do you want? She told me she wanted everything. So I gave her all of me, because that was all I had. - But instead he just answered:

-Let's go to sauna! The Rajaportti one is open until 22:00.-, he thought that he might see Joni.

-I don't have a swimsuit.

-You have a wig. You don't need the swimsuit, everybody is naked.-, he answered, forgetting to mention that Rajaportti is the oldest functioning public sauna in Finland.

A bit later they each got a beer. A bit later cold wind was cooling the hot skin. The lungs were full of fresh air. The breathing was deep, as if they were breathing in the whole world.

Motionlessness, omnipresence between the buildings. Love without motion. Love and belonging. The wind makes smiles of support appear on faces.

The beautiful lamp light in the blinded eyes.

Joni didn't show up.

63
Music

Tampere

Electricity passes through our body at a speed of 12 meters per second
The city lights are made of the Big Bang unrest
Electrons are moving the muscles of the city
Blonde girls are lifting their breasts so that they look better. Ah, the blonde girls
A sound that describes the beauty of life
Somebody is playing a trumpet on Hämeenkatu
Melody is playing with the harmony of desire
People are walking behind the city lights
People are passing by, some stop to listen to the music

Just a second, I need to give students their tickets. You see, we have visitors from all around the world, they love sauna. Of course! Who doesn't love it? Look at that girl getting into the cold water for the first time. See how her friends are taking photographs of her? Funny. We do it for pleasure, not for memories. Okay, you can get pleasure from memories too.

The cosmic fires, a lost groom, an enamoured immigrant - everybody is moving somewhere, everybody wants to create something. Everybody is so obvious, but imperceptible or, to be more precise, incorrectly perceived.

Would you like a shot of vodka? Yes?! You're wonderful.

The cosmic fires create life, the immigrants would like to create life, but whether Panu is ever going to be with Inka is a different story.

Are you interested to know how Botum ran away from the kidnappers? Very easily, you see, because she was fearless like a penguin, and slave keepers operate based on fear, which she doesn't have, which made the escape easy.

65

The Kidnappers in Front of the Room, Botum Inside the Room

-Are they listening to us?-, Botum asked the girl next to her, whispering in her ear.

-I don't think so. Don't eat or drink anything, or you will be drugged.

-They took all my stuff. They gave me only this t-shirt and black panties. What kind of place is this?-, Botum asked.

-A massage parlour. But after the massage, we are expected to give a little bit more.

-I'm running away to the police.

-Don't, they'll kill your family. And they will know soon if you go to the police. They say they have their own police officers.

-I'll escape through the window. I'll take the food and throw it away. You can say that you ate it and that you were drugged, so you didn't see how I escaped.

-Stay. It's not that bad here.

-I'm leaving and I'm not looking back. We're on the second floor. Help me put this sheet down.

-You'll freeze outside.

-We'll see about that.-, she said looking at our funny immigrant stop at the window of the antique records shop. She decided to run to him, because people who like old records are kind-hearted.

Life is very cruel sometimes, and the only way to change it is to not accept its cruelty. No acceptance!

Let's talk about love. Let's see what the friends in sauna are doing. Let's look through the window, it's not steamy now.

The Holy Place

Sauna

You could see through the window that Anna had managed to wrestle out of Aleksi's hug. Not knowing what to do with his hands, Panu walked to the stove and started pouring water over it as if he was possessed. He was shouting:

-Sauna is a holy place! Sauna is a holy place!

-You again, with the holy place. So, tell me, why is sauna a holy place?-, Aleksi was serious.

-I'll tell you why.

-Go ahead, I want to hear something meaningful.

-The most meaningful!

-Anna and Inka, listen to this truth so that you can explain it to Aleksi, because he will not get it.

-Sauna carries the blood of our ancestors. A part of our blood is in this wood.

-It's true.-, Anna confirmed with her lovely smile.

Panu continued:

-We were given birth here, our mothers leaned their feet on those boards. They were lying on those boards when we first saw the light of day.

-That's true!-, Inka confirmed, even though she was born in the town's hospital.

-Our parents fell in love here and made love here.

-That's true.-, it was Aleksi confirming now, when Panu said:

-Here is where Juuso, my dad, was with your mother.-, then he looked towards Inka and continued:

-Here's where your mother was with all the other fathers. Here is where our parents grew up and grew old. Here's where we bathed my parents when they died. Sauna is a holy place.

There was absolute silence; Aleksi was thinking that you don't find anything by sitting, but by moving. Nobody gets anywhere by sitting, but by moving.

-You are so lost in thought. I'll add some water.-, Anna said again with her smile.

The water poured over the scorching stones, all into the same place. It didn't evaporate when she poured some more.

The heat didn't crawl up the walls and onto the ceiling. The heat filled the room with thickness and made it charged.

The water kept pouring. Slowly, into the one same spot over the lava rocks. The bodies understood that the burning ears were just a beginning.

Now everything was burning, even the knees. And the water kept pouring; Anna's calm face provoked incredulity. Then Anna sat on the highest bench in the sauna and said that she loved life and that it was good to live.

-I love life and it is good to live.

Aleksi and Panu lay on the sauna floor, watching Inka and Anna enjoy the heat. They laughed the same way they did when they were children.

-Will you ever go away, Panu?-, Anna asked him.

Panu answered with a wide childlike smile.

Soon, soon, soon. Soon we'll see if Panu will head south. Panu had a fear of changing his environment. Everybody has a bit of that fear, except the doses of fear in him were a bit higher.

Soon we will find if Panu will be with Inka.

Soon our immigrants will head north, on the path towards fulfilling their destinies; there would be nobody and nothing to stop them.

But let me tell you about the musicians, just so that you can connect everything that happened. By the way, I really hate the calm musician, I don't know if I mentioned that. You'll understand why.

Musicians at a Railway Station on the Blue Horizon
New Beginning

The musicians were sitting inside the warm station. The quiet musician was wondering how he ended up inside this station with two morose guys who only lighten up when they are surrounded with beautiful women. The quiet musician realised that he himself was also morose, even though not that expressively. He also realised, which is why I hate him, that he wanted to cheer up with the beautiful woman who was in the sauna, yes, with Inka.

The quiet musician decided to leave, even though he didn't explain it to his friends. He looked through the window; the train arrived at the station. Two people got out, one wearing a penguin costume. They entered the station and said:

-We are looking for Anna and Aleksi. Do you know where they are?

-Aleksi never leaves the sauna. He's there now.

-How can we find the sauna?-, the unmasked passenger asked.

-Easily. Just cross the lake. When you reach the car with 3 frozen Asian guys inside, turn left. After 100 steps you'll find the sauna you are looking for.

-How did they freeze, what happened?

-They were looking for the sauna. They used navigation from a phone they stole from me. They probably got lost, and then they ran out of fuel or the car broke down.-, the quiet musician answered.

-Would you like some vodka, before you head off to the sauna?-, the quiet musician asked.

-Yes, please.-, the unmasked funny immigrant answered and started drinking it like water.

-I can't feel anything.-, he said.

-Go ahead, just drink.-, quietly said the quiet musician.

You could see through the window of the station that clouds were coming, tall and fast, the day becoming dark-grey. The immigrant feared they might get lost.

-I'm afraid we might meet the same fate as those Asian guys.-, he said.

-I can go with you, if you want.-, the musician said affirmatively.

-Of course. Let's go get warm in the sauna.

-Goodbye guys! It's time for us to part ways.-, the quiet musician said to the angry ones.

-You're leaving?-, the angry musicians were not very surprised.

-I'm leaving. Forever!

-What about our thing, our concerts, our saunas, your singing?

-I think you'll manage.

And the quiet, used-to-be Elvis headed across the frozen lake towards his new life.

Towards Lapland

The Train

The immigrants were on their way, it was dark. They were looking for Anna, they were looking for Aleksi. They were on a train, going towards the Arctic Circle, towards Lapland.

-Do squirrels sleep during winter?-, she asked the immigrant biologist.

-They don't, as far as I know, but they don't leave their shelter. They lay around and nibble on the food they collected during summer.

-So, the doughnuts must have been really tasty if that squirrel left her shelter just to go and eat them.-, Botum smiled.

Sleepy and confused, the immigrant looked at the gigantic penguin in front of him. Botum continued:

-That must mean that Anna's doughnuts are very good, if you left your home to be with her.

-The *best* doughnuts.-, he replied.

-We don't have very good doughnuts in Asia.-, Botum shyly mentioned, not expecting an answer, that didn't come anyway.

The train was big; it had two levels, with narrow aisles and narrow berths. It started slowly only to gain speed, in the same rhythm of the tracks and ties. The penguin and the funny immigrant followed the rocking of the carriage. Botum was looking at the dark forest and snow, while the train's lights lit frozen lakes and tree tops. She looked at the burgundy cabins in the light of the train windows and said:

-Just like Finnish tango.

The funny immigrant heard the rhythm, he looked at the dark forest, but he wanted to know what she was really thinking about, so he asked, perhaps inappropriately:

-What is tango, for you?

-For me, tango is mastering the art of feeling sorrow without actually being sad.

-While you are dancing?

-And when I love.-, she replied.

They fell asleep on the cheapest seats leaning against each other, the gigantic penguin and the funny immigrant.

When he woke up it was daytime. The train was rushing between two lakes. On the lake where reindeer had been running and the elk had been scratching the ice, the sun was mirrored now. On the lake where the wolves had been running, people were now skating. Dressed in tight thermal clothing, the people wore warm hats. They skated in a line, in a row. They swung their arms back, while going very fast. The sun was throwing wavy particles of tiny mass, the fast people wouldn't be able to see much without the goggles.

-They are beautiful.-, Botum said sleepily while she was waking up. -Beautiful and fast.

-Beautiful, fast and crazy!-, Botum laughed loudly and closed her eyes again; she seemed to sleep smiling.

She sounded so wise, even though she was joking.

-Why are you so pensive?-, she asked sleepily.

-I'm thinking about wisdom and laughter.-, he replied.

-You and your big topics.-, she said half-asleep.

-You are right.-, he replied.

He was trying to fall asleep. Leaning against the window he was trying to ignore the moving images in his view.

71
For Myself

Tampere

And then my love will come to me
To fill the depth of the universe with colours
Maybe I shouldn't find what I am looking for
Maybe I shouldn't look for others because of themselves
Maybe I should live for myself

Look, the kids went outside to play in the snow. Don't worry, they won't catch a cold, even though they are only wearing shorts. They will go back to get warm if they start feeling cold. Look how beautifully they smile. I don't have children. I am yearning. Look what joyful eyes they have. I'm elderly, I know, it's silly of me to have infantile wishes, but if somebody asked, I'd tell them I wouldn't like to grow up. I'd like to have remained a child always, to warm up in a sauna after playing in the snow, to laugh just because I'm surrounded with other children. Sometimes I have tears of joy when I see children laugh.

Why are you looking at me like that? You want to know when the kidnappers decided to go after Botum? The answer is... immediately. They even saw her once, but they were not aware that it was her.

The Kidnappers and the Search for the Princess

The boss and the workers were sitting in a car parked in front of the train station. The heating was working.

-Don't worry. God sees everything. The elephant will go to its village!-, the boss was comforting his workers.

-Have our people found her family?-, a kidnapper asked a tricky question. The boss had to lie.

-Of course, but we're not going to talk about it now. It's time to look for Aleksi.

-Let's go!-, the boss shouted with a voice full of enthusiasm.

-Look, there at the traffic lights, a gigantic penguin.- one of the kidnappers cheered up.

-Finns are so funny.-, another kidnapper cheered up.

-Is there a reason for that?-, asked the first one.

-That lad is getting married, they are having a bachelor party.-, the boss wisely replied.

-Funny custom. I wish him luck.

-Is this piece of rubbish we're driving going to make it to Lapland?

-We're not far away, only 500 km from the Arctic Circle. The heating is what matters.-, the boss was brimming with knowledge.

What idiots!

But let's change the topic to love and friends in the sauna. What do they see when they look outside the window, what different perspective?

Aleksi knew that the encounter was approaching. Anna knew that the encounter was approaching, which is why she left. Panu knew that soon he would lose his childhood friends, but he had Inka next to him, the materialised object of his yearning.

Let's have a look at what they see outside the window.

On One of the Next Trains

Sauna

You could see through the window that the clouds had collected in the sky and that one of them was very grey. Panu was still lying on the floor and was still laughing, but his look was getting lost in the beauty of the grey sky outside. He thought that life itself was restlessness. He was thinking that the planet itself was alive; it breathes through trees, it moves in its orbit, it looks at us with its sky. Our planet is old and very wise. It even knows how to rejuvenate, with lava eruptions it expels a material that transforms into youth, again and again. Our planet is the third planet from the sun. It orbits in a galaxy called the Milky Way, where birds are looking for their destinations. Our planet is alive, on it we have friends. On it we love, we create new lives. We are the heroes of the Big Bang.

-I'm leaving soon. But before that I'm waiting for Aleksi's future wife to show up. I want to meet her.-, Panu was looking at Inka's face, her lips were smiling; they didn't ask him to stay. They didn't.

-When do you think Botum will come?-, Aleksi asked.

-Soon.-, Panu replied.

-Do you think Joni will come?-, Aleksi asked.

Inka, sitting high up in the sauna, looked at Panu and said:

-Joni is obsessed with spotlights, camera flashes, newspaper headlines, and, in particular, his own abyss. He doesn't talk to others anymore, he only talks to himself. He is not coming back.

-Even though you are not the most normal person, it would be best for you to leave here, for your own good, Panu.-, Aleksi said.

Panu stood up and went outside. The wind started to blow, removing the clouds and exposing a clear blue sky. The snowflakes were flying. The trees were shaking the snow off, as if undressing. The moves resembled dancing, clumsy but pretty. Through the rhythm of nature, Panu spotted three silhouettes approaching.

The first one was a giant penguin.

The second one is coming because of Anna.

The third one was an unwanted guest, he supposed.

A long time ago, near the childhood sauna, on the other side of the frozen lake, inside the train station, Inka pressed her lips against Panu's. She was leaving for Rovaniemi, for good, it seemed.

You're looking at the frozen lake. It's beautiful, isn't it? When foreigners come here and I tell them that the Baltic Sea also freezes over, and that sometimes you can drive the car on that ice, they don't believe it at first, but then they get fascinated when they realise that it's true. You see, fast communication has no use for me. For me the bigger advance is being here with you, maybe that's why I feel privileged to work in this sauna. You see, in old literature people were looking for fountains of wisdom, and now you have the internet. But believe me, it's nicer to come here and talk to people from around the world.

The cosmic fires create events of small probability. The Cambodian woman and the Serbian man met the group of musicians, and thanks to the quiet musician they were on their way to the sauna.

Botum, who didn't want to swim in the cold water before, will soon be swimming in her penguin costume. She'll also see her kidnappers, the frozen monuments. Near Aleksi, who, up to now, was only present through data transmission on the net, she was like a golden bird escaping from the net that covers the whole planet.

Kidnappers Monuments

-God is a being of higher consciousness. He will help us.-, the boss said trying to raise the morale of his workers.

-But boss, it seems that we've been circling for hours.

-Don't doubt God's power, it is absolute.-, the boss returned to his version of the absolute, which was so confusing and abstract that his workers couldn't subvert it.

-Where is Aleksi?-, one of the kidnappers asked.

-He is in the sauna near the railway station.

-Is that the station?-, the second kidnapper asked.

-It is. You see, there *is* universal justice.

Then, resembling bewildered monsters, wearing big beast furs, the dumb kidnappers appeared looking for Aleksi and Botum. They had weapons, fur caps and unsuitable boots, in which one's feet freeze.

-We are looking for Botum!-, one of the kidnappers said.

-Good for you.-, a musician replied, one of the angry ones.

-We are looking for Aleksi! We know that he spends time in the sauna near here.-, the second kidnapper said.

-Why are you looking at your mobile phone? Who are you calling?-, the boss asked, and snatched the phone from the hands of the quiet musician.

-Ahaa! The elephant has come to his village! Look, here is the sauna.

-Great! Great!-, rejoiced the stupid kidnappers with their seemingly smart friend. Then they returned to the car that was still screeching in the cold.

-After 50 meters turn left.-, said the mechanised voice on the mobile phone.

In Lapland

The Train

The cold air was climbing down from the sun with the distance of the universe. In the ether, the warm rays turned completely cold as they were coming down the blue dome of sky. The rays were looking for clouds, to rest on them, but there wasn't a cloud in sight. Cold and beautiful, they landed on the snow, on the treetops, on the lake, the frozen mirror to the sky, on the hot wooden sauna.

Near the sauna, Botum was looking at the sun rays through the train window and realised that she was in love with the light, the forest, the snow, the lake, and Aleksi.

The train arrived at the station. They went outside into the cold. It was so cold that the slightly freezing Tampere temperatures seemed tropical. They came across the musicians inside the station and asked them:

-We are looking for Anna and Aleksi. Do you know where they are?

-Aleksi never leaves the sauna. He's there now.

-How can we find the sauna?-, the immigrant asked.

-Easily. Just cross the lake. When you reach the car with 3 frozen Asian guys inside, turn left. After 100 steps you'll find the sauna you are looking for.

-How did they freeze, what happened?

-They were looking for the sauna. They used navigation from a phone they stole from me. They probably got lost, and then they ran out of fuel or the car broke down.-, the quiet musician answered.

-Would you like some vodka, before you head off to the sauna?

-Yes, please.-, the funny immigrant answered. He realised that the great fear of seeing Anna again was born inside him; he was afraid of rejection, and he was also afraid of a new, meaningful life.

The musicians gave them vodka. The Serbian immigrant felt weak. He took the bottle, hoping that it would spark some courage, then he took a bit more, hoping for some more courage, and even more, to get warm, because he could feel the cold just by looking out of the window. And then some more.

-I can't feel anything.-, he said.

-Go ahead, just drink.-, quietly said the quiet musician.

You could see through the window of the station that clouds were coming, tall and fast, the day got dark-grey. The immigrant feared they might get lost.

-I'm afraid we might meet the same fate as those Asian guys.-, he said.

-I can go with you, if you want.-, the musician said affirmatively.

-Of course. Let's go get warm in the sauna.

They were walking across the lake in the Lappish below zeros looking at the clouds quickly disappear. Soon, after a short time they came across the frozen car with three frozen people inside. A nearly-naked man, wearing only shorts was standing next to the car and showed them where the sauna was:

-Just head left and don't turn at all!-, he looked like a Nordic wise man, but actually it was Panu.

The Serbian immigrant asked:

-What happened to them?

-Surma.-, the nearly-naked man replied keeping the immigrant wondering.

-Are you free now?-, the immigrant asked Botum, who will soon take off her penguin costume.

-I'm free.-, the penguin replied: -Those are my kidnappers. They died looking for Aleksi and me.

They were approaching the sauna, on the spot where the ice was the most slippery, near the hole. They slid and fell into the water, the cold water where sauna people swam.

The cold water wet their clothes, and the immigrants were struggling to swim. The Serbian took off his jacket and tried to see where the others were. He saw the penguin struggle in its black and white suit. He didn't see the musician. The jacket was off now. When he was entering the cold water with Anna, he learned an important truth: you should go out of it fast, but if you can't, then you should breathe very slowly and very deeply. He was already used to swimming in the cold water but he was worried about inexperienced Botum. He was dragging her by her costume, worried that she would not be able to swim.

Then the musician appeared at the edge of the ice and pulled them both out onto the surface.

In My Eyes You Can See the Snow Frozen on the Branches

Tampere

Lamps, streets and thousands of people
The busses are hurrying, my eyes are searching
Around me the locals, the foreigners, the presidents, the champions and drunks with lost souls
And blonde girls
Beauty is in the search
Passion is in the heart
On the bridge between the two lakes
There is a girl on the opposite side
There is a bear on the opposite side
Mielikki, beware of the cold wind
Mielikki, your eyes are harbouring beautiful sorrow
Underneath the blue sky
Among the cold trees
I do remember you, Mielikki

Coming, Leaving

Sauna

After removing their wet clothing, the immigrants were completely naked. Like new-born children, they entered the new world of old friends. In the moments of nudity the funny immigrant became aware of his abs; at least there was some use for so many years of physical labour. He searched for Anna and found her on the top bench of the sauna surprised by the unusual situation. Interestingly, Inka approached him first and hugged him.

Sauna heat was warming the naked bodies quickly, and only then he felt the strength of vodka he had inside of him. All of it, all the alcohol was beating inside. Botum, who didn't drink like him, was shaking. Behind her, at the door, the apparition they saw next to the frozen car appeared. He extended his hand to them and said:

-My name is Panu, nice to meet you!-, he gripped their hands firmly, and without waiting for them to introduce themselves, he asked:

-Where are you from?-, he was looking at the funny immigrant, as if he already knew Botum.

-From Serbia.- he replied and saw Aleksi hug Botum.

-And what's the situation in Serbia?-, Panu's question was sudden, but it didn't surprise the immigrant who was shaken by the alcohol like a tall ship in a storm.

-The situation is very difficult.-, the immigrant replied.

-Why difficult? No jobs?

-Because of women.-, he drunkenly replied.

-Because of women?-, Panu was surprised. Imagine: Panu, surprised!

-The women are hot. The women went crazy. They are so hot they don't leave you alone. In Novi Sad, Niš, Belgrade, Kraljevo, Subotica, Arilje, the women are completely crazy.

It is difficult to exist and stay authentic.

-That doesn't sound so bad.-, Panu went to sit on the highest sauna bench. He was looking at Inka, but she didn't pay any attention to him.

-It may not sound so bad, but the situation is very hard. The women are so crazy that they only think about satisfying their own needs; you are not important to them. You as you, and me as me.-, he saw Aleksi hug Botum, his cold face with warm tears over her shoulders.

-That sounds even better. Maybe I should go to Serbia because of the women.-, he kept looking at Inka who didn't complain about the possibility of Panu's leaving. Instead she asked the immigrant:

-Where is Joni?

-Joni disappeared.-, the funny immigrant said, looking at Inka's serious face: -He fell into the cold rapids and disappeared. The vodka and the heat were about to topple him. He sat next to Anna and said:

-Do you remember how birds flew under the cold bridge in Tampere? They swam next to the frozen shore, below the rapids. They will never fix the world, nor will they heat the winter. Sweet, small, lost birds. They are making love, while above, on the bridge, the heated busses are running, and the people in warm clothes are crossing the bridge without talking.

Anna was silent; her cold face carried warm tears.

The quiet musician was sitting next to Inka like a jolly-eyed yogi; Inka looked at him and smiled each time their eyes met, even though she just found out that Joni had disappeared. Botum, who was shivering, said that they should have a hot shower.

Panu approached the old wooden door and opened it slightly.

-Shame on you! Looking at women who are not yours!-, Aleksi rebuked his friend and walked up to him to enjoy the same beautiful transgression.

Do the cosmic fires care where we are? Botum ran away to the embrace of her love, the funny immigrant was sitting next to his love. Yes, we can see now that Botum and Aleksi are together, but we also see that Inka and Panu will never be together. Panu represents yearning and Inka represents loneliness. Inka, who was so cruelly looking at the musician with her mild eyes. Inka and the new life. Joni had disappeared. The possibility of Panu's leaving didn't worry anyone.

Friends appear and friends disappear.

Inka and Botum were having a shower, the hot water falling down their beautiful bodies. It was sliding down the skinny curves under their big smiles. Panu turned to the immigrant with a tearful face:

-How to get to Serbia quickly, to the crazy women?

The immigrant noticed that Anna leaned against him; happy and half wasted from the vodka and the heat, he said:

-There is an airport in Tampere where you can get a cheap flight to Budapest. From there, it's only 200 kilometres to the south to reach Subotica. Then, go to the centre, enter any cafe and order a gin and tonic.-, he said and saw Inka and Botum return and sit on the warm wood, Inka next to the musician, Botum next to Aleksi.

The immigrant was next to Anna. Panu was looking at the musician and Inka and said:

-I'm leaving.-, he expected that somebody would ask him not to go. He expected that somebody would stop him, but Inka only wished him good luck:

-I wish you all the luck of this world!

Aleksi didn't say anything.

-Do you know how to get to Tampere?-, the immigrant asked Panu.

-By train, I guess.

-Do you know what month it is now?-, Aleksi asked.

-July, probably, or maybe December.

It was hot; they went outside. The immigrant sat on a bench next to the sauna, looking at the blue sky. Anna was sitting to his right, Aleksi to his left. Botum sat next to Aleksi.

-Are you staying?-, Anna asked.

-I'm staying,-, the immigrant said. -But what am I going to do here?

-There is a mine nearby, they are looking for workers. The salary is okay, and after work you have no strength to live, so the costs of living are minimal.-, Aleksi said.

-Great. At least it's not cold in the mine.

The icy water was evaporating off the hot bodies. The cold air caressed the scorched skin. In a small life, inside a heart that wanted to be large, the woman who loved him was leaning against him. They watched the water escape towards the clear skies, towards the low sun, and get lost in the heights, beyond the reach of their eyes. The birds were sitting nearby; tiny, wonderful, lost birds. The wind was coming to play with them. Jolly and fast, it hit their faces. Anna leaned her head on his shoulder and sighed with delight. The wind was playing between their legs. It managed to lift the snow up to the knees. The treetops swayed lightly, the trunks bending in acquiescence. They were looking at the blue, untouchable sky.

Panu was leaving.

While I was walking across the frozen lake I could hear a murmur; children, forest, sauna, heat and cold, they didn't tell me to stay, they didn't even try to stop me. I was walking with determination towards the train station on the blue horizon.

I was leaving. I was leaving, never to return.

Glad to meet you.

Yes, *I'm* Panu.

I'm glad you came, really glad. Now you know.

84
The Train

I'm leaving now, even though it's July
I'm leaving now, even though it's December
I'm leaving now, on the same road, but in different
directions
On the other side of the glass there are
advertisements
Products that are not for me
Nobody is holding me, because I am nothing
Nobody is waiting for me, because I am nobody
It's warm
It's cold
I'm leaving now
Now I'm leaving with a smile

Now you understand why I hate the quiet musician. Now you understand that only funny immigrants would send you to their own country to have a gin and tonic; that's why I called him funny.

Year after year - a hundred, year after year - a thousand, year after year - a million, year after year - a billion, and like that, sixteen times. Sixteen billion years have passed since the Big Bang. I'm sure you understand that I had to leave. I left my spot, I left my village! Inka paid more attention to that musician than to me. She gave me nothing. I left and I still love her. My love is eternal. My yearning is eternal.

It feels really good, telling you all this. I'm relieved. I've confessed. This was somehow a religious act. Thank You.

Would you like a shot of vodka? Yes?! You're wonderful! I rarely drink, and only vodka. I've changed, I don't drink beer anymore.

You've heard the story, my story about the yearning of a broken-hearted man, the story about an immigrant from Serbia, about an infamous acrobat, about friends and musicians from Lapland and about a fearless girl from Cambodia who connected them all.

I went to Serbia then, via Budapest with the cheap airline. When I was on a minibus to Subotica, inside that climate-controlled box, I met some musicians who were travelling to a village near Subotica, to a music festival. They invited me to go with them and I agreed; the only things I needed were a café and a gin and tonic. I expected mountains in Serbia, but what I saw were the plains and the sunset of a tall sun. The musicians went to rehearse for their festival, and I left them and went to a café and ordered a gin and tonic. I was in a new environment, surrounded by people who were drinking beer.

Beer was cheap, even for the locals, while gin and tonic was expensive, fifteen times more expensive than the beer, but still cheaper than the average price in Finland. I was in a new environment and feeling agitated. I was ordering more, just to dull my emotions. I was looking at women, but they weren't crazy, they were jolly. I was feeling sick. After many gin and tonics I ordered a beer and that's when the emotional flat-lining happened. The flat line wasn't the most pleasant, in fact it was awful, which is why I don't really drink beer anymore.

Then a smiling girl approached me. She had lovely almond eyes and lovely chestnut hair. She took some ice from the bucket at the bar and washed my face. She was like Inka - imperfect, insecure, fragile and unique, unsurpassable, absolute.

But she wasn't Inka.

I returned to Finland, but not to my village. I got a job in Tampere, in a sauna.

Yesterday my friends came, and one enemy, the quiet musician.

Botum and Aleksi have three children. Botum looks just the same as when I saw her in Lapland, as if time hasn't passed. The children get their good looks from her. Anna and the funny immigrant have two children. Luckily they are pretty like their mother, and they have that lovely smile, just like their mother's. Inka and the quiet musician, my great enemy, came with a girl who looks like Joni and with two other children who look just like my enemy. Love, sorrow, nature and sauna.

I was looking at the children play in the sauna. They bathed together, playing with a bucket of cold water on the floor. Wonderful children, I could see their parents in them, just like our parents saw themselves in us, in our sauna.

I'm glad you were here. When you come to Tampere to the sauna again, when you ask for a ticket and look into my blue eyes, you should know that there is sorrow in them because I am yearning; if you see something in my eyes, know that those are the tears that tell the story of my eternal love.

Thank you for coming.

Thank you and come again.

Part II

The Brave Young Woman

Seemingly unconnected with the previous part, this part is actually essential, maybe even primary.

This part is a story about a young woman who wasn't just fearless but was also brave. About a woman who got to know her fears and fought them. Yes, brave women know their fears and that is not easy.

This part of the story talks about people of good will who helped the brave woman to be brave.

And the brave woman gave them a gift in return; soon you will know what it was.

87

Aino

Aino lived in a one-storey house. She was looking for her cross country skis, but she couldn't find them. She checked every single corner of the storage room. She found the ski boots and the poles, but she didn't find the skis. From the storage room, she went on to check all the other rooms of her home. The walls of her bedroom were covered with violins and guitars of different sizes, postcards and posters of snow covered mountains. Behind the window it was snowing, behind the falling snowflakes, there was a forest. She saw her father sitting in the living room, reading a book. He wasn't her biological father, but he was a better father than any of you could imagine. Her mother wrote poems about the beauty of the snow. Nobody ever published her poems, but her mother enjoyed telling herself how beautiful the snow was.

When she looked through the snowflakes, she wanted the skis to take her to another side of the world, to the sea's fragrant shore. She wanted to be free, in the salty water under the sun. But she couldn't find her skis. She was in the corridor when the phone rang.

-This is Aino.

-We'll be there in half an hour. Be ready, we're doing twenty kilometres today, then after that we'll go to the sauna.-, it was her friend.

-Ok. I'm waiting for you.

-Is your boyfriend coming too?-, the friend asked.

-I don't know, you ask him. You can come together, if he wants to.

Next to the Window

Aino put on the warm wide boots and her coat. Unbuttoned, she walked to the nearby pharmacy. She was there for a short time and went out of the warm place back into the snow-decorated day. She buttoned up her coat this time. Even though she was already sixteen, she still looked like a ruddy little girl. Large snowflakes were falling on her blonde hair. She walked slowly and carefully. She went back inside her home and stopped at the mirror next to the window. The snowflakes were falling on the white road; the snowflakes were falling on the white trees. A young woman was passing near the window, pulling a sled. A smiling girl was sitting on the sled; she could've been around one or two years old. Underneath her cap she had curly hair and red cheeks. Aino looked at her own cheeks in the mirror next to the window; they were equally red. The sled was leaving tracks on which the snow kept falling. The little girl turned to the window and waved. Aino waved back and greeted her with a smile.

The Conversation

She returned to the corridor. She decided that she didn't want to look for the skis nor did she want to find them. Her heart started beating like a steam engine. She breathed heavily, and she was trying to calm down. From the corridor, through the window she watched the snowflakes and the empty white street. She entered the living room where people who loved her, her non-biological father and biological mother, were sitting.

-I'm pregnant!-, she said loudly.

At that very moment her mother was writing a poem about the beauty of snow. Her pen slid to the side of the page, running away from the sudden statement.

Her non-biological father was more cool-headed. He promptly asked:

-Do you want to keep it?

-He has already left. The father of the child... he is not in Finland anymore, he's not even in Europe.

-Do you want to keep the baby, Aino?-, her now calmer mother asked.

Aino looked through the window, through the snowflakes, through the forest. As if she didn't want to abandon that pensive look. She didn't reply.

Red Cheeks

The doorbell interrupted the view through the window to the forest; it rang for a long time. The non-biological father let the Aino's friend and boyfriend in. Aino was standing in the living room. She had a serious face, with red cheeks. She was as pretty as a flower. In the warm home, in the cold Finnish winter.

-I'm pregnant.

-Are you sure?-, her boyfriend, named Juuso, asked, while holding onto the wall.

-Very sure.

-But we were never together that way.

-I'm very much aware that we were never together that way.

Aino's friend was looking at her parents, who were looking at their daughter, realising that Juuso was not the father. The friend wanted to help Aino, so she said:

-Let's go. The rest of the gang is waiting for us in the coffee shop next to the track.

The News

A little later Aino met her friends. They were sitting in the warm coffee shop. Juuso was wearing a nice ski suit, his face serious, but he was quiet and decent. Aino dropped the news to her friends:

-I'm pregnant!

-Are you sure?

-I'm very sure; there is no doubt about it.

-You already managed to get pregnant, and I haven't even found a boy who will even touch me.-, one of the girls said; nobody doubted that Juuso was the father.

-Are you going to keep the baby?

-I don't know.-, Aino replied.

-What does Juuso say?

-Juuso doesn't say anything, mostly.

Aino was looking at her friends; they were pretty. They also had cheeks as red as flowers. Outside, boys were skiing in their nice special suits, on very good skis, among the butterflies made of frozen water.

Freedom

When Aino came back home, her mother and father were waiting for her, and they were waiting with hugs. The mother gave her smiles and tears beneath her calm gaze. Aino shed tears in the hugs, tears that were salty on her lips.

When the hugs loosened and the looks went the other way, Aino went to her room and lay in her bed. She was looking through the window when she dialled, and another phone rang in Argentina.

-Hi, it's Aino. How are you? Nice. I'm okay. I'm pregnant. I know you are only twenty. I don't know if I want to keep it. I want you to know that you are free. Why don't you want to see me?

The conversation was short. A chandelier hung from a thin cord from the ceiling. Aino considered ending her life on that cord then started crying. She thought how the life inside her was more important than herself.

Support

Aino was lying in her bed when her mother came in. The two women lay on the bed next to each other. The mother put her hand over her daughter's hand. She was silent. Aino was content, because, other than tears, she also needed company and silence. She could hear her mother's breathing, she felt her gentle hand, and she felt the warmth. She looked through the window; it looked as if the snow fell everywhere so that nature could be warm.

-Who is the father of the child?-, the mother quietly asked.

Even though the silence disappeared, Aino was not dissatisfied.

-A musician from Argentina. Actually, he's originally from Uruguay.

-How did you meet him, my child?

-I met him after the music festival. He was playing *candombe*. I was playing the violin and guitar to his drums. It was all my idea. Now he doesn't want to see me.

-It's easy to be strong when everything is okay. The real strength comes when we stand up after our defeats.

The snow was falling, it was warm and cold. Aino was crying, both happy and sad.

Special

The school corridors branch out to many different parts of the world, they have many doors. Aino was studying music in the conservatory and she was a very good student. Children are opening and closing the doors, big children pretending to be adults, big children leaning against the corridor walls. Aino was walking along the school corridors, and everybody knew that she was expecting. Everybody! The janitors and the superintendent, the teachers and the principal... everybody. Aino was special and she felt special. Aino was unique. The big children who leaned against the walls looked at Aino.

-Bravo, Aino.-, the boys were saying.

-Bravo, Aino.-, the girls were saying.

The teachers were getting away, just like Juuso. The teachers were not saying anything, because they lost their youth a long time ago.

95
The Decision

Aino was walking along the white street. Aino was walking next to the white forest. Aino was walking along the school corridors. Aino was walking in her home. Aino was walking.

When she sat in front of her biological mother and non-biological father, she told them:

-I want to keep the baby.

-You are a brave girl,-, her mother said.

-You are a brave young woman.-, her father said.

Aino called her friend who then called the rest of the friends to tell them about Aino's decision.

It was snowing outside, the snowflakes were hurrying through a seemingly ordinary day, but no day is ordinary, Aino realised, no day; every day is special.

The Phone Receiver

There was snow, it was daylight. There was a phone call:

-Juuso, is it you? Jusso, why are you silent?

-It's me. I'm not silent, see?

-You avoid me at school, you avoid me outside school. Why are you silent?

-I'm not silent.

-Do you know that I decided to have the baby?

-I know.

-How are you, Juuso? Why are you silent? I feel so alone, so weak.

-I know.-, Juuso said and then he went silent and kept silent.

-I think it's time we break up, Juuso, and to stop having what we perhaps had.

Aino put down the phone receiver violently, and it slipped from the hook and dangled by the cord. There was snow, it was daylight. There was a phone and the sound of a hung up phone receiver, beeping to the rhythm of the sobs of a brave young woman.

97
The Plan

The wind ran through her hair, impermanent, expected, caressing the surface of the rippling lake. Aino had a plan on how to meet the Argentinian boy, she had a plan on how she would sit on him, and everything went according to plan. In the moment of passion, Aino wanted to become pregnant and it all went according to plan.

Now, while she was walking back home, Aino was planning what to do with her life and her studies. She was grateful to her parents for making such a great home for her and helping her secure such life.

Couples were hugging and young parents with small children were passing by the round Aino. The children were happy and beautiful like the green summer, like the loud birds, like the wind on the surface of the lake.

Courage and Goodness

While she was standing in front of the mirror in the corridor, she thought how she started looking like a ball with small legs. In the window next to the mirror, the Finnish summer could be seen, nature blooming green, girls wearing short sleeves and short skirts, boys taking off their shirts to show how strong they were. Some mothers and some fathers were taking their children to blue and green lakes, to the big and small beaches. The scent of sunscreen was entering through the window, the birdsong, the flight of the butterflies who danced around the couples in the warm day, in peace, in light.

Her parents were sitting in the living room when Aino entered.

-Hello, brave young woman.

-Hi Mom, hi Dad. I just had a look at myself in the mirror; I'm turning into a ball.

-There's only a little time to go. Then a little baby is coming to us.-, the mother said.

-Are you going to look for a job?-, the mother asked.

-I was thinking about it.-, Aino said.- I will continue living as your child and as a young mom. I'm not going to drop out of school. I'll continue my education, and then I'll decide if I want to go to university. I'll find a part-time job to cover my costs.

-Smart, brave, young woman!-, the non-biological father said. -You have an excellent way of thinking. Enjoy your youth and your new role.

-My smart child!-, the mother hugged Aino. Both of them were crying tears of joy next to the open window, through which the cheerful smell of summer was entering.

99
Maternity Clinic

She walked through the green summer underneath the blue sky, through lines of trees and parks, along the lakes and beaches, by the people, couples and children. She was walking alone to the maternity clinic.

The nurse was explaining to the mothers-to-be the process of dilatation, and proper nutrition, showed them the delivery rooms, and the showers next to them. She showed them the beds for new mothers and cribs for new-born babies.

-I just want the child to be okay! I just want my baby to be born healthy!-, Aino thought out loud when she was leaving clinic.

It doesn't matter who will love me, I don't care what other people are going to think, and it doesn't matter if it's a boy or a girl.

The birds were swinging on the branches. The wind was fast, it was swinging the branches and treetops that were shining in the bright daylight.

100
With Friends

They were sitting on the bed and around the bed. The friends were wearing colourful clothes, the blonde friends with red cheeks.

-So, what was the Argentinean like?-, one of the friends asked.

-He was wonderful that evening.-, the ball-like Aino answered.

-Do you miss him?-, the other friend asked.

-I don't miss him. I don't even know him. I miss Juuso, his attention and his tenderness. His *goodness*.

-Juuso is probably angry. I would be very angry at you myself; I wouldn't even want to see you.

-Thanks for your support!-, Aino joked.

-But Juuso *is* looking at you; he just pretends he is not.

-Juuso. Soon he will become a man too.

-And we will become women.

-*Women*. Funny.

101
In the Park

She was walking on the green grass looking at the birds flying low. She reached the lake upon which small boats were gliding. On the other side there was a playground full of children; swings and see-saws, merry-go-rounds, slides. And a sandbox.

She was stroking her basketball-like belly. She was surrounded by life and by children. She lay on the grass looking at the sky; she thought how the universe was alive.

She was happy. Happy. Happy.

102
At the Doctor's

-Eat well, walk a lot. Do you eat well?
-I do.
-Do you walk too?
-I do, every day.
-Good then! Keep it up. Is the child kicking?
-Yes it is. As if it was dancing.
-Great! Healthy child. Dancing in the belly.
-Will I know when the time has come?
-You will. You'll be sure.

The hospital walls were white, but warm. Aino was leaving there with her parents. She was grateful to have everybody with her, only Juuso was missing.

103

Aino and Jusso

Aino and Juuso met in the street, surrounded by couples, children and warm summer. Juuso was riding his bicycle awkwardly when he stopped in front of her.

-So you decided to greet me?

-Hi Aino. A little time to go!

-It can happen any moment. That's why I never go too far from home now.

-I heard that the father is from Argentina.

-You heard well. I miss you, Juuso.

-I miss you too, Aino.-, Juuso said and left, meandering awkwardly with bicycle among the summer people.

The Delivery

It seemed that the summer would last forever. Aino was with her parents when her water broke. Her mother kissed her gently and said:

-Let's go, brave young woman! Let's go, my pride and joy.

Her father was driving her to the hospital, to the delivery room that she had seen. She was on the bed feeling very strong contractions. She thought that she could not control her own muscles; she thought that nature was out of her control and that everything that was happening was meant to happen. The muscles were contracting on their own; the nurses were coming and giving her pain killers and infusions. The time passed by in the contractions; she was not afraid.

When the baby was born, they lifted her so that Aino could see her well, then put it on her bosom.

-A girl! My girl!-, Aino was shouting, tenderly touching the new-born.

The nurses bathed and swaddled the new-born. Aino had a shower and lay on the bed that was assigned to her. Next to her bed, in a small crib, they lay her child.

Aino was exhausted. She was lying watching her beautiful girl. Juuso entered the room, without saying a word. He lay behind Aino and hugged her. They both cried looking at the little child, they cried of happiness and sadness, together as if they were dancing tango.

Aino gave the girl a name later.

The girl was called Inka.

***

Aino was growing up together with Inka and took pictures that documented her growth. When she finished high school, she looked at herself with a baby in her arms, she looked at herself when she became a teacher, and she looked at Inka in framed photographs when they moved to a village near the train station on the blue horizon.

You could see Inka's joy in the photos. Inka was always smiling, but she was becoming so restless that neither cameras nor videos could capture her truly.

Part III

Children

The third part is short, but very wise, although it does not pretend to be wise. In it are the children, maybe those children who were playing in the sauna. With their simple language they say what adults don't know how to say, or what the adults try to say with music and dance.

106
Sorrow

What is sorrow?
I'm not sad.
But sometimes when you are sad?
Sorrow is when I am sad because I have to go to sleep.
What else is sorrow?
Sorrow is when good people die.
Who are good people?
Good people are those who love us.
What else is sorrow?
Sorrow is when parents are angry.
Because life is to love.

Happiness

What is happiness?
Happiness is when my parents kiss me goodnight.
Happiness is when I laugh a lot. When I see something funny.
Happiness is when I am surrounded with a lot of girl friends.
What about boys?
Boys are dumb.
What is happiness?
Happiness is when everybody is laughing.
And for you, boy, what is happiness?
Happiness is when you love.
Happiness is when my parents hug me when I am sad.

108
Love

What is love?

I don't like chicks.

Ok, boy, you are still young. Tell me, do you know what love is?

Love is when you love.

And for you, girl, what is love?

Love is when you love somebody who doesn't have a lot of stuff.

What do you mean?

Love is when you love somebody because they are good and kind, and not because they have a lot of stuff.

What else is love?

Love is when we play hide-and-seek.

Love is when we are running and laughing.

Love is when they read goodnight stories to us.

Love is when we are with our friends.

Love is when we dance.

About the Author

Boško Velimirović was born in 1972 in Serbia. He spent seventeen years living abroad, first in Spain, where he worked mostly as a bartender, then in Finland, where he works with people from more than sixty countries in an IT company. He has had three novels published in Serbian. Finnish Tango is his fourth novel, and his first book available in English.